T0107623

# Code Name Pigeon

## Book 6: Homeland Security

### Girad Clacy

iUniverse, Inc.
New York   Bloomington

## Code Name Pigeon
## Book 6: Homeland Security

*Copyright © 2009 by Girad Clacy*

*All rights reserved. No part of this book may be used or reproduced by any means, graphic, electronic, or mechanical, including photocopying, recording, taping or by any information storage retrieval system without the written permission of the publisher except in the case of brief quotations embodied in critical articles and reviews.*

*iUniverse books may be ordered through booksellers or by contacting:*

*iUniverse*
*1663 Liberty Drive*
*Bloomington, IN 47403*
*www.iuniverse.com*
*1-800-Authors (1-800-288-4677)*

*Because of the dynamic nature of the Internet, any Web addresses or links contained in this book may have changed since publication and may no longer be valid. The views expressed in this work are solely those of the author and do not necessarily reflect the views of the publisher, and the publisher hereby disclaims any responsibility for them.*

*ISBN: 978-1-4401-2384-9 (pbk)*
*ISBN: 978-1-4401-2385-6 (ebk)*

*Printed in the United States of America*
*iUniverse rev. date: 3/9/09*

# Dedication

*This final book in the Code Name Pigeon series is for you, Adriaan. You allowed me to take the simple idea of a book series and turn it into a reality. May you never grow old, may you remain forever young.*

*Girad Clacy.*

SPOT Agent Michael Pigeon

# Chapter 1

Michael was resting comfortably in bed at home when the phone started ringing. He slowly opened his eyes and looked at the alarm clock next to the bed. It was 10:15 am and already someone wanted to talk to him. He simply ignored the ringing of the phone. He closed his eyes and went back to sleep only to have his cell phone start ringing. He knew then that it was Bill Yancy or one of his designated representatives calling. Michael rolled over in bed, sat up and grabbed the cell phone, which he had carelessly placed on the nightstand next to the bed when he was sent home from the hospital.

The cell phone stopped ringing and when Michael was awake enough to see the display, he saw that the message symbol was illuminated. Michael went through the motions of checking his message. He decided to call the office back because the voice mail message had been labeled as urgent. He dialed the office-restricted number. The person who answered the phone there told him to come in for a priority mission briefing. After hanging up the phone, he managed to muster enough energy to get out of bed and get dressed. He looked at his watch, which told him he was due for another dose of painkiller. He took the dose and went on into work via the Light Rail System.

Michael Pigeon, having survived his injuries during the previous mission, was in another mission briefing. As he tried to concentrate on the issues at hand, the massive amount of painkiller he had received only an hour ago was taking its toll on him. His mind was swimming and his reactions were severely slowed up. Little did he realize that this would be his last mission. The mission briefing was being held in conference room six. When he arrived, there were pictures of missiles being launched and missiles in flight being shown on the screen.

The Secretary of Homeland Security had briefed Bill Yancy. Bill had been told that, despite the best efforts of the diplomats and the Central Intelligence Agency's clandestine branch operatives, 450 Al-Fatah II missiles were unaccounted for. Libya had denied, at first, that they even had the upgraded missiles. Then Libya went on to say they had made a few hundred and sold some of them to various Middle Eastern nations such as Iraq, Iran and Syria.

The Central Intelligence Agency had accounted for 30 of the Al-Fatah II missiles as having been sold to Iraq, who renamed them an Al-Samound II missile and Syria had some. Syria decided that the missile was far too big for peaceful defense purposes. The Iranians denied having any of the missiles and called the former Libyan president, Muammar Al-Qaddafi a liar. They cited the fact that they had purchased the missiles, but that the Libyans had never delivered the promised goods.

According to the best military intelligence sources, the Al-Fatah II missiles were capable of carrying a 2,000-kilogram payload to the intended target. Along with the possibility, due to a more stable platform, it could carry a chemical, biological or even a tactical nuclear warhead with an estimated size of 500-kiloton. These newer missiles were more of a threat because they could be launched from almost any type of missile launcher such as the SCUD, Frog-7 or the older Al-Fatah I missile. These newer missiles were capable of longer ranges as well.

These factors, put together with the discrepancy of the Libyans having made over 500 of the Al-Fatah II missiles and only being accounted for 30 of them, made this mission a double-header for Michael. Michael soon realized that he might have to protect the United States from the missiles at all costs. Michael pulled a notepad out of his pocket and started to take notes.

Michael found out his mission was far more than a double-header. This mission was three-fold. First, how many of the Al-Fatah II missiles were actually manufactured. Two, where are those missiles now and finally, at all costs, transmit the location of those missiles so that they could be destroyed by U.S. or Allied assets in the area. Michael realized that this would probably be his most dangerous mission. After the briefing was over, Michael raised his right hand so he could ask some questions.

"Yes, Michael, what is it?" asked Bill.

"Bill, could the records have been falsified?"

"That is one possibility. That could account for any of the missiles that were test fired into the sea or into the desert."

"Do the Libyans have any underground bunkers that we don't know about?"

"No. Our intelligence reports say that we know all of the locations of Libya's military hardware, training facilities and other targets of interest."

"Then, how did we miss that many missiles that are in a country that we know everything about?"

"We don't know, that's why we are sending you there, to find out what the story really is. Among other things, make sure that if you see any of these missiles that you try and get the serial numbers off of them. The serial numbers are located on the right side of the fuselage between the upper and lower tailfin assemblies."

"What's the angle I'm using?"

"You're a journalist for a military identification book publisher. You want to get some pictures and information on these missiles for your book publisher, which is me."

"Sounds reasonable. Who's my point of contact?"

"A major within the Libyan Army. He is in charge of the missile defense system that Libya has. He is also a CIA clandestine operative, so be careful."

"I will."

"Good, I look forward to your first report."

"When do I leave?"

"Tomorrow evening."

"Guess I should go home and get some sleep then. Where's my stuff at?"

"It will be waiting for you at the airport under your name."

"What nationality am I supposed to be?"

"Austrian."

"Understood."

Michael left the briefing room and went home. He took another dose of his painkiller. He looked into the bottle, only one more dose left. He went to bed, after packing, and slept until the middle of the afternoon the next day. He went to the airport, checked through security and boarded the first of four planes. As the plane took off, Michael took the last dose of his painkiller.

The plane landed in New York at John F. Kennedy International Airport. Michael switched planes and ended up sitting on the ground for almost an hour and a half before taking off. He slept the entire trip to Paris, France. After getting off the plane, he had about six hours before the next flight.

He stretched out as he entered the airport, yawned and looked around for a coffee shop. After clearing customs and having his passport stamped, he found a coffee shop just a few gates down from where he was. He walked sluggishly at first; the painkillers hadn't worn off just yet. As he moved closer to the coffee shop, he could smell it. Michael ordered a large, dark roast coffee and sat down to drink it.

He stretched out once more in the coffee shop and reached into his pocket. Grabbing his pager-looking device, he turned it on to check for any urgent messages; he found none. He turned it back off and went back to drinking his coffee. The next time he looked down at his watch, he noticed it was time to start wandering towards the gate where his next flight would depart from. His watch automatically calibrated for local time via radio signals. Locating a teleprompter, he found he was pretty close to the next departure gate and he soon joined the rest of the passengers in boarding the flight.

The flight took off and soon Michael was boarding the last plane in Rome. That plane took off and as the plane circled around the city and headed out to sea, Michael wondered what kind of person the CIA clandestine operative was going to be. He had seen a picture of him during the briefing so he could recognize him when he stepped off the plane. The flight went smoothly and the plane touched down in Tripoli, Libya at dusk. The moment Michael stepped off the plane, the heat of the desert day hit him like a good solid punch from a professional boxer.

Michael walked into the Tripoli International Airport and was soon met by the CIA operative. He shook Michael's hand and greeted him warmly. Michael noticed that he was wearing his military uniform and that his rank was indeed major. The major looked around and quickly escorted Michael to customs. Michael opened up his bags and camera cases for the inspector and handed the inspector his passport. As the inspector looked at his camera equipment and clothes, the major dropped a small roll of Libyan Dirham's into the camera case. The inspector looked up at the major.

"Diplomatic pouch, inspector," said the major.

"Yes, sir, major. Welcome to Libya, Mr. Pigeon and I hope that you will enjoy your stay," the inspector, said handing Michael's passport back to him after having stamped it several times.

Michael closed up his camera cases and his suitcases and put his passport in his left, front pocket. Walking out of the airport, the major pointed to his military vehicle, which was parked out front of the airport. The Land rover® was painted in a desert camouflage scheme. Michael noticed that the major wore two guns and at least six magazines for each of the weapons. One gun was strapped to the major's left thigh and one on his right hip. As Michael put the last of his luggage into the vehicle, he spoke to the major.

"That was a neat trick in customs. I would never have thought to call my camera cases and underwear diplomatic pouches."

"Privileges of rank. Now, come along, you must be hungry."

"Yes, I am."

The major and Michael stepped into the vehicle and they drove off. At first, the major drove through town, then he went up a hill, then back down the hill on the opposite side. Then the major did a series of other maneuvers that Michael recognized as trying to lose a "tail" as they were called. The major finally drove through a crowded market area of Tripoli and off into the desert. After awhile, Michael decided to strike up a conversation with the major.

"How did you become the new missile defense commander?" asked Michael.

"I inherited the position when my commanding officer, General Al-Hambarh Ali-Barhaba, committed suicide in the office one night. He shot himself in the back of the head while on his knees."

"Any witnesses?"

"Ten other people in the offices around him. Everyone heard the gunshot, but no one saw anyone go into or out of the office."

"Okay. What's the plan now, major?"

"When we get to my place, we will talk then."

The major drove across the desert at high speed on a road that was only paved a short distance. The rest of the trip out to the major's house, the vehicle left a large cloud of dust behind. After over an hour or so in the vehicle, they arrived at the major's house. He helped Michael with his cameras and luggage.

Michael noticed that the major's house was built on top of a small hill. As he looked around it, there would be almost no way anyone could approach the house without being spotted. Michael looked up at the roof of the house and noticed what appeared to be old machine gun posts on each of the four corners of the house. He merely nodded his head in agreement with the configuration and stepped inside. When

Michael walked into the living room, he saw that the inside of the house was totally different from the outside.

As Michael looked around the living room, the living room had several odd recessed places in the wall. Michael thought they looked like a design he had seen in England once on a castle. The design was to allow someone that was on the inside of the recessed place in the wall a way to shoot out and not receive any return fire. The person, who was in the living room or any of the hallways leading to the guest rooms, would be taking the bullets or arrows, depending on which weapon was used. The hallways going to the various guest rooms were angled out from the living room area. The kitchen was totally separate from the living room as was the dining room.

The major showed Michael a luxurious room facing the north towards a high set of sand dunes. To the south, Michael noted rocks and more sand. In any east/west direction, it was up the hill to the house. Yes, this was definitely the Sahara for sure, even if it wasn't the middle of it. After dinner, Michael and the major sat down in the living room to talk. Before they started talking, Michael brought out one of his "cameras" and set it on the coffee table.

Michael turned on this camera by the shutter speed adjustment button. Soon a red flashing light on the camera by the shutter speed adjustment button alerted Michael to the presence of possible eavesdropping equipment. Michael reached into his camera case and withdrew what looked like a roll of film. The roll of film was actually the other part of the camera.

Opening the top of the roll of film, Michael looked at the red LED lights to tell him which direction to go. He looked at the major and motioned for silence. The roll of film pointed out to Michael four electronic eavesdropping devices in the major's house. After Michael had disabled these devices, he went back to his camera case and put the roll of film and camera back into the camera case.

He reached into the camera case, pulled out another camera and set it out on the table. Michael reached down and turned this camera on. The red LED light started flashing once again. Michael grabbed a piece of paper and wrote a message and showed it to the major. The message said, "We are being monitored by a laser transmitter/receiver. Where can we talk without being monitored?" The major pointed his right index finger down. They soon headed for the basement of the major's house. Michael noticed that the basement was actually a small bunker.

"How did you end up with a bunker?" asked Michael.

"It was left over from when General Rommel was in this part of Northern Africa during World War II."

"I see. What is the game plan?"

"I will take you in the morning to the main plant where the missiles were made. You will be escorted at all times by me. Speak to no one, I'll do all the talking except if they speak directly to you."

"Okay. I should get some sleep then."

"I will see you in the morning."

Michael went to bed and slept well. The major told Michael that he would let his contacts know that Michael had arrived so that others would not worry about him. The major also prepared for anyone becoming too nosey with his Austrian visitor.

# Chapter 2

There were gray storm clouds hanging over the entire city of Norfolk, Virginia. Sitting pier side at Pier 4 was the newest member of the nuclear powered U.S. Navy, *USS Grand Junction* CA-144. The ship was the first heavy cruiser the United States Navy had had in over 40 years. Her gray hull and superstructure blended in well with the current weather pattern.

The ship was totally redesigned. Based off the heavy cruiser class *Des Moines*, the *USS Grand Junction,* was devoid of the 20mm and 40mm anti-aircraft guns. The newly redesigned ship had replaced them with anti-submarine rockets and the close in range weapons system or CIWS as it was called. However, the ship still maintained her triple mounted, single turret, 8-inch guns. There were two forward and one aft. The guns were still capable of firing 21 rounds a minute.

The open spaces created by the removal of some other equipment allowed for vertical launch tubes in the forward and aft decks for both TOMAHAWKS and HARPOONS. The ship also carried the newest member of the torpedoes, the Mark-50 Advanced Capability, heavyweight torpedo. These new torpedoes allowed a ship to use one torpedo against both surface and subsurface targets. The ship carried a newly designed AEGIS combat system to assist the crew in handling their multi-level mission.

The ship carried a smaller crew than the original heavy cruisers of 40 years ago. The ship was also about 1,100 tons lighter than her predecessors. However, she still retained the unmistakable armor belt around her waterline to protect her vitals such as the reactor rooms, engine rooms and magazines. As the sun tried to beat through the thick cloud cover, the exterior of the ship was silent.

The interior of the ship, however, was starting to bustle with activity of all kinds. Sailors were starting to wake up. Some were shaving while others were taking showers and going to eat breakfast. Some went to relieve others that had been on various watches since 0400 hours, for breakfast. The officers were milling around the wardroom waiting for breakfast as well. The captain and the executive officer were in the captain's stateroom going over the results of the previous underway time. The captain was reviewing the section on "shock trials" when the announcement tone sounded.

"There are divers working over the side. Do not throw anything over the side. Do not activate sonar or any other underwater electronic equipment. Do not take suction from or discharge to the sea or vent or blow any tank. Do not rotate screws or cycle rudders without first contacting the diving supervisor and the chief engineer."

To everyone on the ship, that meant that repairs to the ship were still underway. The shock trials, according to the Naval inspectors, had done some damage to the rudders, propellers and various other pieces of engineering equipment. A few minor injuries to some of the sailors below waterline were also reported. Although injured, the ship was still capable of doing her job and getting underway if necessary. There was a knock on the door to the captain's stateroom.

"Enter!" barked the captain.

A radioman, first class petty officer, entered and saluted both the captain and the executive officer. He carried in his left hand the morning message traffic. He handed them to the captain and departed.

The captain reviewed the messages and handed them to the executive officer for dissemination. They both stood up and went to the wardroom for breakfast. The announcement tone sounded again and the same announcement was said again. The captain looked around the table to find the chief engineer missing.

"Where's the chief engineer?" asked the captain.

"She's been up half the night with those divers over the side trying to get the port rudder fixed," replied the main propulsion assistant.

The chief engineer entered the wardroom a few minutes later. She looked tired and stressed out. She had in her hand the report from the divers about the rudder and the starboard outboard propeller.

"Glad you could join us, commander," said the captain, sarcastically.

"Sorry, sir. I was waiting on the final report from the divers. Here it is," she said, handing over the report.

The captain reviewed the report and put it with the other report going to the Commander of Destroyer and Cruiser Squadron Six, Admiral Atwell.

"How long to replace the starboard outboard propeller?" asked the captain.

"About eight hours, sir. The Norfolk Naval Shipyard is sending a couple of tugs with a crane for the divers to put the new propeller on. The crane should be alongside in about half an hour."

"Why do we need a new propeller? Do we even have one available?" asked the executive officer.

"According to the divers, our starboard outboard propeller has a cracked dunce cap and is approximately eight inches off center from blade tip to blade tip. Thankfully, there was no damage to the shaft, otherwise we would be in dry-dock right now, sir. To answer your other question, the Norfolk Naval Shipyard has received the new propeller from the Newport News Shipbuilding and Dry-dock Company. The port rudder was easily fixed by realigning it."

"Good. Weapons officer, what is our weapons status?" asked the captain.

"We have no weapons other than small arms, flare and chaff charges and active and passive decoys for torpedoes. We need all other weapons."

"Okay. Operations and all the other departments seem to be okay according to their reports. Medical officer, how are those injured sailors doing?"

"Doing well, sir. I have returned them to partial duty. I expect, unless there are complications, that they will be on full duty by the end of the week," she replied.

"Good. What's for breakfast?"

He waited a few minutes after breakfast before going back to his stateroom. Upon arrival, his government issued cell phone started to ring. He picked it up and looked at the caller ID. The caller ID told him it was Admiral Atwell calling him. The captain answered the phone.

"Good morning, skipper. Can you come to my office?"

"I can be there in 20 minutes."

"I'll see you then."

The captain hung up the cell phone and put it into his left pocket. Grabbing his Eisenhower jacket, he put it on and called the executive officer to his stateroom and turned the ship over to him. The captain departed and went to Admiral Atwell's office. Only Admiral Atwell and the captain knew the contents of the meeting, but upon returning to the ship, the captain readied the ship to get underway for immediate sea training.

The gray storm clouds had started to loose their heavy load they were carrying. With the rain falling down and visibility reduced to almost zero, the ship set the sea and anchor detail. The harbormaster told the captain that the next high tide would be about 1830 hours.

At 1845 hours, with several tugs alongside, the ship was pulled out into the harbor. With the forward motion of the ship, the rain was coming down even harder. The captain had the bridge windshield wipers turned on. Once the ship had cleared the last tunnel and was heading out to the Chesapeake Lighthouse, the captain turned around to look at the illuminated skyline of Virginia Beach disappear into the foggy night.

# Chapter 3

The next morning, Michael woke up feeling ill. He wasn't doing much better after breakfast. However, by the time he was taken to the missile manufacturing facility, he was feeling better. The major showed his ID to the security officer at the front gate who just waved him on through. The major parked the vehicle and Michael stepped out. The air-conditioned vehicle that he had been riding in only moments before was replaced by the stifling heat of the desert day.

Michael grabbed a pen and a notepad along with his real cameras. Quickly he loaded them with film and followed the major inside the building. To Michael, the outside of the building was rusty and filthy looking. In fact, Michael could see where the rust had run down the outside of the building in certain places and had left rust stains behind. However, when Michael stepped inside the building, the building took on a whole new life. The inside was unique.

Michael walked into what he thought was a surgical ward. The place was brightly lit and air-conditioned. He looked around not finding a single speck of dirt, dust or lint anywhere. This impressed him as he scanned the rest of the entryway to see a long hallway in front of him.

He could see the major talking to someone at the end of the long hallway. The major motioned for Michael to come down the hallway to where he was standing.

As Michael walked down the hallway, he looked right and left with his eyes only. He was being careful not to look directly at something for fear of drawing unnecessary attention to himself. He noted that there were rooms with doors down two hallways to his right and left. Michael smiled as he approached the two men. Michael pulled out his notepad and pen as the major spoke to him.

"Mr. Pigeon, this is Mohammed Ali-Akbahar III. He is our principle missile person and was personally responsible for the development of the Al-Fatah I and II series missiles," said the major proudly.

"Could I take his picture, major?" asked Michael, as he put up his pad of paper and pen.

"Sure," replied the major.

Michael snapped a few pictures as the man said something to the major. The major turned to Michael.

"He hopes that you got his good side!"

They all laughed at this. The man turned to Michael and spoke as he opened the double-doors at the end of the hallway. When the doors were fully opened, Michael stepped into an area that provided him with all sorts of photographic opportunities.

As far as the eye could see, there were missiles, missile parts and launchers in the building. The assembly area was further labeled clearly with large signs which missile was being assembled in which section of the building. All sorts of missiles in all stages of assembly were present as well. Michael went to take pictures, but was stopped by the major.

"I want to take some pictures, if that's alright with you, major," said Michael.

"That's alright with me. However, Mr. Akbahar here wants to show you how proud he is of his accomplishments, first," said the major, winking his right eye at Michael. Michael caught on to this right away.

"Okay."

The major and Mr. Akbahar walked down a narrow catwalk to the far end of the building. There, Michael began taking pictures of the various assembly lines. The man showed and talked at great length on how the Al-Fatah I and II series missiles were made.

The man went on to explain that, unfortunately, some years ago, Libyan President Qaddafi told him to put the assembly line in preservation and release his workers. The man did it and although it was by presidential order, Michael could tell the man was deeply saddened by the order. For right now, Michael was writing down all the information the man was willing to give him for his "story." Michael knew this information would be most helpful to Bill back at the "publishing" company.

As they proceeded down the various assembly lines, Michael took more and more pictures. After the interview was completed, the rolls of film were to be sent to Austria via a special delivery service to the "publisher." Michael knew that the pictures were to be sent to Bill. A copy of those pictures would be sent to the Department of Homeland Security and the Central Intelligence Agency for analysis and filing.

Michael was still writing when they came to an area of the building that the man asked that no pictures be taken. Michael agreed happily as he turned on his camera that were built into his fake glasses. To turn on the camera, all Michael had to do was press firmly on both sides of the frame like he was readjusting them on his nose. The pictures would be transmitted to a small DVD recorder located in the bottom of the camera case. Those pictures would be sent off tonight as well to the same places. The place they entered was a small weapons laboratory.

The man told Michael, as Michael wrote down as much as he could, that this weapons experimental lab was used in the early 1990's to test the feasibility of putting chemical or biological payloads on the Al-Fatah I series missiles. He went on to explain that experiments were failures, but that this lab had been cleaned when the plant was shutdown in 2003. The next room over had not been cleaned when the plant closed and turned out to be even more impressive.

Michael saw the radiological symbol on the door as they entered. When they had walked inside, Michael felt hot all of a sudden, even though the building was air-conditioned. This experimental weapons lab was, as the man explained, used to test the feasibility of putting nuclear warheads on the Al-Fatah II series missiles.

Michael knew that he couldn't ask a blunt question to get the information, so he asked the major the question. After the tour ended, Michael wanted to get more information about the missiles themselves. The man smiled again and went into his office. He returned a short time later with pictures of both missiles and a brief synopsis of their capabilities.

Michael thanked the man for his time. The major thanked the man for his time as well. Michael thought the man seemed overly cooperative to talk to him and the major. When the major and Michael were back inside the major's house, Michael used the major's computer to send the pictures. Using the major's scanner, he scanned all the information packets that the man had supplied them. That night, after dinner, Michael and the major went down into the bunker.

"I didn't think your country had nuclear weapons," said Michael.

"I didn't think we did either, however, I was not always privy to every project my commanding officer was involved with," replied the major.

"I understand. Where did all those missiles go?"

"I don't know. Tomorrow, you and I will go to one of three missile testing facilities and see what we can find."

Meanwhile the photos and information packets had arrived. When the photography section decoded the pictures, something odd showed up on them. The pictures were clear, but each one had either a halo or spots around the edges or in the middle of the pictures.

When the pictures arrived on Bill's desk, he looked at the halos and spots with some concern. He thought he had seen this photograph oddity somewhere before, but he couldn't remember where. He picked up the phone, as he set the pictures down on his desktop. He was calling the Department of Homeland Security.

"Good morning, Sam Mallory, can I help you?" he asked.

"Sam, this is Bill. Did you get those pictures from Michael?"

"Sure did. What caused all those halos and spots?"

"I don't know. I was going to ask you the same question."

"I don't know, either. My people are analyzing the pictures and information packets that Michael sent. We should have results by the end of the week."

"Okay, then, I will be expecting your call."

"Good-bye."

The line went dead as Bill called his Central Intelligence Agency contact.

Meanwhile, Michael was feeling ill once again. This time it was much worse. He felt "hot" all over and he was vomiting violently. He felt better after a cold shower and some breakfast.

Michael wasn't to realize until some time later, that he and the major had been exposed to a lethal dose of radiation. This was all part of a carefully devised plan to eliminate both of them by Libya's new president. The new president was planning on attacking the United States with Al-Fatah II series missiles. Each one of those missiles was carrying a 500-kiloton tactical nuclear warhead. He was planning to inflict more civilian causalities than Osama Bin Laden had inflicted with his attack on September 11, 2001.

# Chapter 4

Michael had the major stop several times on the way to the missile testing facilities. Once they arrived at the first missile test facility, Michael put on a smile and loaded up his cameras for the tour. The major escorted Michael into the first of three buildings on the facility site. The major introduced Michael to the facility engineer. The engineer wore a uniform similar to the major's but without any type of rank identification.

The major, Michael and the facility engineer started the tour by going into the large warehouse they were inside of already. When Michael stepped through the set of double-doors, he stepped onto a large platform. Below Michael were several Al-Fatah I series missiles. At the far end of the warehouse were several of the Al-Fatah II series missiles. As the tour progressed, Michael put on a large telephoto lens onto one of his cameras.

The facility engineer escorted the major and Michael to within 20 to 25 meters of the Al-Fatah I series missiles. Michael took lots of pictures of these missiles with the facility engineer standing proudly by them. Michael moved the camera around for a couple of shots. Then

Michael switched to the other camera and took some pictures of the Al-Fatah II series missiles. Michael was using the large telephoto lens to capture the serial numbers on those missiles. Michael was remembering that the serial numbers were located, according to the mission briefing, between the tail fins on the right side.

The facility engineer took Michael to the next warehouse. Michael and the major were shocked to find more Al-Fatah II series missiles. There were numerous launchers for SCUD's, Frog-7's and Al-Fatah I series missiles, which Michael was pretty sure weren't accounted for during the 2003 inspection. Michael counted at least 75 to 100 of these Al-Fatah II series missiles. As he took more pictures, the facility engineer took them all to the third warehouse.

This warehouse housed a tracking facility for when the missiles were launched. Once launched, the tracking facility would be able to track the missiles in flight. Michael took lots of pictures of this facility. The equipment seemed like it was in almost perfect condition for being in a state of preservation. Michael then noticed the large satellite dish and some peculiar equipment that was in one of the rooms.

The major thanked the facility engineer for his time and they drove off. This time, to get something to eat and drink before reporting to the test firing facility. The test firing facility was several hundred kilometers to the east of Tripoli, near the Mediterranean Sea. When the major had refueled the vehicle, the major drove Michael to the facility. Michael looked out the window of the vehicle at the desert terrain. Again, Michael had to ask the major to stop several times.

They arrived at the test firing facility at about 1645 hours local time. The sun was still up and there were only two buildings on the property. Again, a large satellite dish with three smaller dishes around it, were outside the first building. The major parked the vehicle and Michael stepped out, stretched and grabbed his cameras once more. The facility engineer came out to greet them. Again, the same basic uniform as the major's, but without any type of rank identification. Michael was expecting the major to interpret, but was surprised by the

English spoken by the engineer. Michael wondered how someone could learn English in a part of the world that didn't allow such things.

"Mr. Pigeon, welcome to Libya's Missile Test Firing Facility," said the engineer in English, with a heavy accent.

"Thank you. I would be very interested to know all about what this facility does, for the sake of my readers and the publisher," said Michael.

"Right this way," replied the facility engineer, pointing to the first building.

Michael, the major and the facility engineer stepped into the building. Michael noted that there were several large radar screens and a map of the missile range hanging on the wall. The map showed a large area in Libya for test firing the missiles. Michael must have stared at it too long, for the facility engineer spoke to him. Michael looked at the map again, this time at the map's orientation to the rest of Europe.

"Our test firing range map, Mr. Pigeon."

"Seems large," said Michael trying to come up with a reason why he was staring at the map.

"It is very small compared to, say, the United States' Test Ranges."

"How much smaller?" asked Michael, trying to get the information he wanted without being too direct about it.

"Quite a lot smaller. There are missile test ranges in the United States that are 4 times the size of ours. This one is only 600 nautical miles in size. 100 nautical miles out to sea and 500 nautical miles to the south into the desert."

"That makes sense," replied Michael, dryly.

"Makes missile recovery prospects excellent. The missiles either crash at sea in shallow water and well within our territorial waters, or they crash into the desert."

"You have salvage operation capacities?" asked Michael.

"Yes, we do. However, since we no longer test any missiles, the salvage equipment is gathering rust sitting pier side at the Tripoli docks."

"My readers would like very much to know, as close as you can tell me of course, what the range is on those missiles?" asked Michael.

"Our tests have confirmed, give or take a few nautical miles, of course," started the engineer.

"Of course," interrupted Michael as he wrote all this information down.

"The Al-Fatah I series missile has a range of between 950 to 1,100 nautical miles."

"My readers are going to love this technical stuff," said Michael, egging on the engineer's ego.

"The Al-Fatah II series missile is estimated, because of it's larger size, to have a range between 1,125 to 1,300 nautical miles."

"Very nice, sir. I would like to thank you for your time."

"It's been a pleasure and when can I get a copy of this book?" asked the engineer.

"I'll make sure to inform my publisher to print you up an advanced copy for your bookshelf."

Michael and the major left the facility. As the sun was setting, Michael dozed off. He was resting comfortably when the major awakened him. They were at the major's house. Michael downloaded the information and the pictures. Next, he bundled up his notepads and prepared them for shipment. Michael and the major went down into the major's bunker once again to talk after dinner.

"Major, did you look at that map in the missile test firing facility today?" asked Michael.

"No, I sure didn't. Is there something wrong with the map?" asked the major.

"That map was oriented to the southern coasts of Portugal, Spain, France, Sicily and Italy."

"Meaning what, exactly? I'm not following you," said the major, very confused.

"If you were to extend out the map to, say, 1,100 nautical miles, you could see how many targets you could hit. Cities like Madrid, Spain, Rota, Spain, Niece, France, etc."

"In other words, my country has a unique missile range," was all the major could conclude.

"Okay, here's the scenario. Your country wants to attack a NATO country as part of a coordinated plan with other Middle Eastern countries. Your country launches several dozen missiles and then claims that the missiles went out of the missile test firing range accidentally. Think of how many civilian casualties you would have from a missile landing its 2,000 kilogram payload in a major city at lunchtime."

"I had not thought of that scenario."

"Well, the computer is done and I'm tired."

As Michael was taking a shower that night, a large chunk of his hair fell out. Michael looked at this and made a mental note to see about it when he got back to the United States.

The next day, Michael went with the major to yet another missile facility. This facility was supposed to be for storage of the missiles to be used during an attack on another country. This building was along the waterfront. Michael and the major had no trouble getting onto the piers, after the major dropped some money into the guard's hands. They drove up to a gate that was chained shut. After the major opened the gate and drove through, Michael went about loading up his cameras. Once the major had parked the vehicle, they both stepped out of the vehicle and walked up to a locked, metal door.

The major opened this door and he and Michael walked into what appeared to be the storage facility. Only the facility was more like a massive records vault. There were no missiles at this facility. The major turned on some lights and went back to where Michael was standing. Michael was looking at the ship docked next to the building.

"That ship is an old cargo carrier. I've never seen her sail," said the major.

"Yeah, you're right. She doesn't look too seaworthy to me, either. I thought this was supposed to be a missile storage facility; this looks like a large records vault to me."

"I noticed that myself. Perhaps this is the storage vault that my commanding officer was talking about that contained the information on the missiles. I wonder what we will find."

"I don't know, let's start looking around."

As the major and Michael started looking around the boxes, the pictures were received, along with the notepads, in Bill's office. Bill immediately sent the pictures to the Department of Homeland Security and the CIA. As Bill sat back to eat lunch, his cell phone rang.

"Bill, how soon before you can be out here to D.C. for an emergency meeting?" asked the CIA director.

"Has something come up?"

"Yes, now when can you get here for the meeting?"

"I'll call for the Department's jet. I can be there in 3, maybe 4, hours."

"Good enough."

Bill hung up his cell phone and called the airport. The hangar crew rolled the executive jet out onto the tarmac. As the hangar crew waited for Bill to arrive, the plane was fueled up. A few minutes later, Bill was aboard. The jet took off and 3 hours, 47 minutes later, he was touching down at Washington-Dulles International Airport. As Bill stepped off the plane, he could feel something wrong even before the black limousines picked him up. Bill stepped inside the second one and was taken to CIA headquarters.

Once he was at CIA headquarters, the Secretary of Homeland Security met him. They both walked down the hall from the front desk check-in. They walked all the way to the end of the hallway where they entered a small room. Bill took his seat opposite the Director of the CIA and to his left, the Secretary of Homeland Security. Two other people were at the far end of the table standing between a movie screen and projector. The lights were dimmed and the first of many pictures was put up on the screen.

"Mr. Secretary of Homeland Security and Mr. Bill Yancy, Department of State's Director of the Special Projects and Operations Taskforce," started the woman standing to Bill's left.

There was a pause as all the pictures were put up on the screen one after the other. The halos and spots were present in all of them including the new pictures just received only hours ago.

"We have isolated the cause of the peculiar patterns on the pictures we received from Michael. These next pictures will be of similar type with similar irregularities," she said.

The next sets of pictures were taken from the late 1960's and into the early 1980's of various places where nuclear weapons had been tested or detonated. Most of the pictures showed the Nevada and New Mexico deserts in the background with the peculiar halos and spots.

"It is with some regret we have to tell you this, Mr. Yancy, but those pictures your operative sent back are the direct result of exposure to gamma and X-ray radiation of very high levels."

"What?" exclaimed Bill.

"Yes. The particulars are these levels of gamma and X-ray radiation is associated with the presence of weapons grade Plutonium without proper shielding."

"So my operative was exposed to radiation, I don't get it," said Bill.

"Mr. Yancy, he was exposed, in the few minutes he was in that room, to a near fatal, or fatal, dose of radiation. In fact, both operatives may be exhibiting the terrible symptoms of radiation poisoning."

Bill leaned back in his chair and then realized that the mission he had sent Michael on would be his last.

"Oh, God. How long do they have?"

"A few weeks, maybe only days. What concerns us more here is, how did the Libyans obtain weapons grade Plutonium, what did they use it for and where is it now," said the Secretary of Homeland Security.

"I didn't think the Libyans had the capacities to produce weapons grade Plutonium. How did they get it," asked Bill.

The Director of the CIA looked at the man standing to Bill's left and merely nodded his head at the man.

"We have a theory that either the nuclear generating facility in Tripoli or their breeder reactor they built for peaceful purposes was able to produce minute quantities of weapons grade Plutonium. Weapons grade Plutonium is Plutonium with an atomic mass unit rating of 249," said the man.

"Their nuclear program appears outwardly to be peaceful enough, however, we cannot overlook the real possibility that the Libyans may have produced a nuclear device," said the Secretary of Homeland Security.

"Do we have such proof?" asked Bill.

"Not as of yet. According to the United Nations Weapons Inspector's report in 2003, Libya abandoned its chemical, biological and nuclear weapons programs," said the Director of the CIA.

"It would appear that you received the latest pictures from Michael," said Bill.

"Yes and it appears by those pictures that the Libyans did produce a substantial amount of Al-Fatah II series missiles," said the man.

The first set of pictures showed the missiles all in neat rows. The next set of pictures showed the serial numbers of as many of the Al-Fatah II series missiles as Michael could take pictures of without drawing unnecessary attention to him.

"Those serial numbers do not appear on the weapons inspector's reports. Those missiles were probably made prior to 2003 and must have been hidden away somewhere. If you look at the next set of pictures, you will see some interesting things," said the man again.

The next series of pictures showed how the missiles were to be assembled. The next set of pictures was taken at the experimental weapons lab. The pictures showed there once were operational devices used for making and testing chemical and biological weapons. The last set was about to be shown.

"Do we know if they were successful with their experiments?" asked Bill.

"We know that they were supposedly unsuccessful in their experiments. We have incomplete reports that the Libyans couldn't get their Al-Fatah I series missiles to fly right with the chemical or biological payloads," said the woman.

"What happened during those tests?" asked Bill.

"The missiles they equipped with the payloads flew very erratically. Normally the Al-Fatah I series missiles carry a 500 kilogram payload about 1,000 nautical miles. This distance makes the missile an intermediate range ballistic missile or IRBM, for short," said the woman.

"Jesus Christ, that missile could hit almost everything in Africa and definitely well into Europe," said Bill.

"Yes, sir. However, the new and improved Al-Fatah II series missile is 40% larger than the Al-Fatah I series. The Al-Fatah II series missile has an estimated range of 1,100 to 1,300 nautical miles. Still within the IRBM status category, but not far from ICBM capacities," said the man.

"Oh, God," mumbled Bill.

The last series of pictures showed the crude devices in the next lab over. The devices were old and outdated, but the man decided to explain what they were.

"In the beginning of our nuclear weapons era in the early 1940's, devices, such as you see pictured here, were used to make the first atomic bombs. The people who built those bombs, because of lack of good equipment and proper shielding, all died of radiation poisoning symptoms. Much better equipment was developed a few years later which increased the safety factor," said the man.

"Tell me more about the Al-Fatah II series missile," said Bill.

"The Al-Fatah II series missile normally carries a 2,000 kilogram, high explosive, reverse cone shaped charge. Since the missile is larger, it can fly with less problems with an unbalanced payload," responded the man.

"I see, Mr. CIA director, could you produce a weapon of mass destruction with this archaic equipment?" asked Bill.

"No, Bill. The equipment is designed for small nuclear warheads," he replied.

"Oh my God, sir. What is, theoretically, the largest nuclear warhead you could put on one of those missiles?" asked Bill.

"Theoretically, a 500 kiloton, tactical nuclear warhead could be fitted to the missile without reduction in performance or range," said the woman.

"What could you use a 500 kiloton tactical nuclear warhead for?"

"You could use it to slow up ground troops or you could use it as a bunker buster. The warhead could carry a reverse cone-shaped charge and be detonated just a few feet above the ground where the bunker is at," said the woman.

"Why detonate the weapon only a few feet above the ground? Why not ground impact it?" asked Bill.

"If the tactical nuclear warhead is to be used as a bunker buster, then detonating it a few feet above the ground would be optimal. The resultant shockwave created by the detonation would simply implode a bunker even if it is buried up to 30 feet in the ground," said the man.

"I think you two should call an emergency meeting with the National Security Advisor to the President," said Bill.

"Why?" asked the Director of the CIA.

"Don't you see? If these missiles are real and all that equipment is real, the Libyans have achieved nuclear status," said Bill.

"I hope they don't plan on using these tactical nuclear warheads against civilians. That is against Geneva Convention Protocol and could result in an ugly retaliation from us and our allies," said the Secretary of Homeland Security.

"No, I don't think they would use them against us or civilians, but they could use them against military bases around them which would cause us a slower reaction time to the threat," formulated Bill.

"I'll call the meeting. Do you think we need to go to threat level Orange?" asked the Secretary of Homeland Security.

"No, not yet. I would wait until something more concrete comes through from our respective operatives," replied Bill.

Meanwhile, Michael and the major were both showing signs of exposure to radiation. Neither one wanted to admit it, but the major suspected it was radiation poisoning after the symptoms set in as rapidly as they did. It pained the major to think that his country either tried or had developed nuclear weapons for attack purposes.

# Chapter 5

The major and Michael had been poring over documents for the past two days. The nausea was getting worse and now fatigue had started to set in. Michael noticed that the major was almost as sick as he was. Again, both of them dismissed what was happening to them as stress or some other reason. Michael was rubbing his eyes and looking at the old cargo carrier outside the window. It was then that he saw someone walking around on the decks that faced the window Michael was looking out. The person was armed with an AK-47.

"Major, if that ship is such a rust bucket, why did I just see someone walking around on the decks with an AK-47?" asked Michael.

"I don't know, maybe to keep out thieves, perhaps?" was the major's answer.

"Yeah, probably. What did you find?" asked Michael.

"I found receipts for the purchase of the Al-Fatah I series missiles as well as those for the Al-Fatah II series missiles."

"Who's buying?"

"The list is pretty extensive, but the top 10 are Syria, Iraq, Iran, Sudan, Bolivia, Mexico, North Korea, Japan, Ecuador, and Mexico. It appears that the Chinese only purchased one."

Michael thought it was strange that Ecuador, Mexico and Japan would be purchasing these missiles. Then his mind wandered to why the Chinese only purchased one.

"Why did Ecuador, Mexico and Japan purchase these missiles?" asked Michael.

"I don't know why Ecuador or Mexico would want a missile with the capabilities that the Al-Fatah series II missiles have. Japan could want them in case they had to fire on North Korea. The missiles would have enough range to reach the capital city," answered the major.

Michael thought about it for a moment and it seemed militarily plausible that Japan could use the missiles, but Ecuador and Mexico was still sending up red flags.

"Major, how many missiles did Ecuador and Mexico buy?"

"Ecuador purchased 100 of the missiles. Mexico purchased only two and one for the Chinese."

"Okay, I'll buy that for now. Why did the Chinese only buy one?"

"Museum piece perhaps?" responded the major.

"Alright, let's take a break, I need to go to the bathroom."

A little while later, Michael was looking at the cargo carrier again. Rust stains were everywhere; the white paint on the superstructure and the bridge areas was stained rust red. The black hull was showing signs of rust as well.

The mooring lines were weather beaten and looked as if, at anytime, they would break. Green slime could be seen hanging off the lines. With the break over, Michael and the major went back to looking over the records.

"Major, how many missiles were purchased total by all countries, not just the top 10?" asked Michael.

The major flipped through the paperwork and counted the number up.

"According to the records, 650."

"Did your country deliver?"

"Yes, the records indicate that the missiles were delivered."

"Something is not right, here. If your country delivered all those missiles, then logically there should have been none for us to photograph. Yet, there were plenty to take pictures of."

"You're right about that, it does seem strange."

"If your country delivered these missiles, then when did they complete the delivery?" asked Michael.

"According to the records, the day before the United Nation's Weapons Inspectors arrived. That's really an odd time to deliver all those missiles."

"Or maybe it's just really convenient. Major, we have to fax this information off right away."

"That's taking a big risk if it's intercepted," said the major with some concern in his voice.

"I realize that, but this information is too important to pass up."

Meanwhile, half a world away, the Secretary of Homeland Security was just getting off the phone with the National Security Advisor to the President. The National Security Advisor had given the Secretary a couple of pages of questions that needed to be answered before the briefing that was to take place later on that evening.

The National Security Advisor instructed the Secretary that he was NOT to increase the threat level to Orange without proper documentation or a directive from either the National Security Agency or the President directly. With list in hand, the Secretary looked over his phone list, locating the number to the Director of Intelligence for the continent of Africa. Quickly he dialed the number.

"Intelligence Branch Africa, can I help you?"

"Yes, this is the Secretary of Homeland Security. Who is in charge of Northern Africa Military Intelligence, specifically Libya?" he asked.

"That would be Geoffrey Tomlin, sir. However, I will send Dan Hamber instead."

"Why?"

"Geoffrey Tomlin is a man with a bachelor's degree and an idiot."

"Well, be that as it may, I still need him. Whether he is an idiot or not, that is your own opinion. I need Geoffrey to report to briefing room four in five minutes."

"Yes, sir. However, still be prepared for an idiot."

The Secretary hung up the phone and went down the hall to briefing room four. He waited for Geoffrey Tomlin to show up. While waiting, he set the sheets of questions down on the tabletop.

At the end of the table were several television monitors. The technicians in the room were loading up various pictures of various types of missiles that the Libyans were known to have and some others that they didn't have. Geoffrey showed up, entered and faced the Secretary of Homeland Security.

"You wanted to see me, sir?" asked Geoffrey, hesitantly.

"Yes, I did. I understand that you are the resident expert on Northern Africa Military Intelligence, specifically Libya."

"Yes, sir. I have all the latest information, as of last week, that is, on all Northern African nation's military forces and capabilities."

"Good. Can you tell me what those three pictures are on the middle set of screens?"

Geoffrey turned around and readjusted his eyeglasses. He stared at the middle set of screens then turned back to the Secretary. Geoffrey took in a deep breath.

"The screen on my left shows an Al-Samoud II series missile. Classified as an SRBM or Short Range Ballistic Missile. The middle screen shows an Al-Fatah I series missile. Classified as an IRBM or Intermediate Range Ballistic Missile and the right screen shows an Al-Fatah II series missile also classified as an IRBM. The Al-Fatah II series missile is not far from ICBM status."

"Good. What are their capabilities?"

"The Al-Samoud II series missile is a short range ballistic missile or SRBM as it is classified by the military. It carries a 500-kilogram payload. The missile is very common in both the Middle East and Northern Africa. The Chinese developed the missile and I believe that the missile is based off of the Chinese SILKWORM missile technology.

The Al-Samoud II series missile was used against Kuwait by the Iraqi military when we ousted Saddam Hussein in 2003."

"Very good, I am most impressed. Could you put a chemical, biological or nuclear warhead on that missile?"

"Chemical and biological, yes, as long as you maintained the weight ratio; otherwise the missile would tumble in flight. A nuclear payload is possible. The maximum size, due to space and weight constraints, would be approximately 100 kiloton."

"A tactical nuclear warhead only, or could it carry a weapon of mass destruction?"

"Only a tactical nuclear warhead. The Al-Samoud II series missile was not designed to carry a large payload. In fact, the missile could be very easily used, if tactically nuclear armed, as a bunker buster to destroy bunkers buried 5 to 10 meters underground."

"Okay. What about the other two?"

"Both the Al-Fatah I and II series missiles could carry chemical and biological warheads. The Al-Fatah I series missile is not capable of carrying a nuclear payload. The missile is equipped, however, with a larger explosive payload consisting of a 1,000-kilogram, high explosive, reverse cone-shaped charge. The Al-Fatah II series missile, due to its larger size, normally carries a 2,000 kilogram payload of the same type."

"Could the Al-Fatah II series missile carry a nuclear payload?"

"Yes, sir. It could carry a tactical nuclear warhead of 500 kiloton maximum."

"What are the ranges of those missiles?"

"The Al-Samoud II series missile is between 100 to 125 nautical miles. The Al-Fatah I series missile is between 950 to 1,100 nautical miles and the Al-Fatah II series missile is estimated between 1,100 to 1,300 nautical miles."

"How are the Al-Fatah missiles controlled?"

"They are controlled by gyrocompass. However, you could use a form of radio frequency homing as well."

"Radio frequency homing?"

"Yes, sir. Radio frequency homing was a project that Hitler was working on during World War II. His Nazi agents in the U.S. had delivered to him the operating radio frequencies of the FM radio stations on the east coast of the U.S. He had formulated plans, with Admiral Doenitz, head of the German Navy at the time, to put a ship to sea with the newer V-3 series rockets aboard. When the ship was close enough to the east coast, the missiles would be launched and after they were in flight so many minutes, the missiles would seek out their pre-programmed FM radio station in the chosen major U.S. city."

"You said these V-3 series missiles would use the FM radio station frequencies?"

"Yes, sir, that was the plan, but neither the missiles nor the plan went into effect due to Hitler's demise and the allied invasion of Germany."

"Is that list of frequencies accurate today?"

"No, sir. A lot of those radio stations don't even exist anymore. Plus, the list only went from 88.4 Megahertz to 99.4 Megahertz. Today, our FM radio stations are on the dial from 88.4 Megahertz to as high as 108.3 Megahertz."

"How easily could you fool one of those missiles with this radio stuff aboard?"

"Very easily, sir."

"What type of launcher would you need for these Al-Fatah missiles?"

"The Al-Fatah I and II series missiles can be launched from either an Al-Fatah I launcher, for the Al-Fatah II series, a SCUD launcher, an old Soviet Frog-7 launcher or any straight steel girder assembly. All you have to do is make sure that there is a good blast deflector plate under the missile for launch."

"Okay. Let's say, for instance, that one of these Al-Fatah II series missiles is equipped with, say, the maximum nuclear payload and is launched at Miami, Florida, downtown section. What kind of damage can I expect?"

"Is the missile going to be a ground impact or airburst?"

"Ground impacted."

"There would be a 1 kilometer kill zone where nothing would survive. From there out to 5 kilometers, any structure that is not made of reinforced concrete or steel, like a bunker, would be damaged by the heat and shock waves. From there out to about 15 kilometers, flash burns and heavy radioactive fallout can be expected."

"So what you're telling me is, the effective zone could go out as far as 20 to 25 kilometers from ground zero?"

"Yes, sir."

"Thank you for your time."

"Yes, sir."

That evening the Secretary of Homeland Security briefed the National Security Advisor to the President on the issues at hand. The National Security Advisor said he would pass along all the information to the President for his final decision. At this time, however, the National Security Advisor decided that no threat level increase was warranted due to the lack of what was termed "credible or specific threat information."

The fax arrived on Bill's desk. He reviewed it, making sure that the fax went to the CIA and the Department of Homeland Security. After this was completed, he picked up the phone and called the United Nations. His call was routed to the United Nations U.S. ambassador.

"What can I do for you, Mr. Yancy?" he asked.

"Who did the nuclear power plant and breeder reactor plant inspections on Libya in 2003?" Bill asked.

"That would have been headed up by the International Atomic Energy Association in Paris, France. The weapons inspectors reported that the Libyans have no nuclear program as of 2003."

"I understand that, sir. However, what about prior to 2003? It is conceivable that they may have constructed or tried to construct nuclear warheads for their missiles."

"The report shows that they didn't have a program. If you don't have anything further, I need to get on with my day."

"Yeah, there is one more thing. Find out why the Ecuadorians bought 100 Al-Fatah II series missiles and the Mexicans bought two

Al-Fatah II series missiles and get back to me on that!" said Bill, angrily, as he slammed the phone down.

After that phone call, Bill decided to call an old friend of his at the University of Colorado in the Physics lab.

"Hey, Bill, good to hear from you. What's on your mind?" asked Joseph.

"What types of nuclear reactors can produce weapons grade Plutonium?"

"We have several here in the U.S. The French have one, the Commonwealth of Independent States has six or seven and some breeder reactors can. But, you have to have the right equipment or else it is deadly to the personnel making the stuff."

"How much do you know about nuclear weapons?"

"Very little. I know that the payload is a shape charge of Plutonium 249 and it is a highly controlled substance everywhere in the civilized world."

"How much weapons grade Plutonium would you need to make a tactical nuclear warhead?"

"Not much at all. In fact, you could have your reactor plant make it and probably slip it passed the U.N. detectors. This could be easily done if you were clever enough to hide the right equipment in, say, a false wall near the reactor building itself."

"Thanks, we should have coffee someday."

"Sounds great; good-bye."

Meanwhile, the new Libyan President was finalizing his plans to launch an attack on the United States in retaliation for the capture of his comrade Saddam Hussein and his summary execution by the new Iraq government. The new Libyan President was briefing the captain of the ship. The captain of the ship was made to understand that him, nor his crew, nor the ship would come back from this mission to protect the Homeland.

The captain understood that he was to "kill as many of the infidels as you can." The ship was heavily armor plated and very well maintained on the inside. Her cargo holds, forward, amidships and aft, held a total of 450 Al-Fatah II series missiles. The cargo holds were lined with blast deflector plating.

Each missile was pre-programmed with the operating frequencies of FM radio stations all up the east coast starting in Miami, Florida. Each missile was also equipped with a 500 kiloton, crudely made, tactical nuclear warhead.

Michael and the major were at the major's house when Michael realized why they were sick and what they were sick from. Michael realized that after loosing more hair and now teeth were starting to fall out, that they both had been exposed to radiation and were suffering from radiation poisoning. He went into the major's bedroom and woke the major up. The major opened his eyes and looked towards Michael as the major turned on the light that was sitting on the nightstand next to the major's bed.

"Major, do you remember that second experimental weapons lab we looked at?" asked Michael.

"Yes."

"Did you notice anything on the door before we entered?" asked Michael.

"No, not really, why?"

"Major, we are suffering from radiation poisoning. Don't you see? Your scientists died making nuclear warheads without the proper equipment or shielding. That room we were shown was heavily contaminated with radiation."

It was at that time the symbol on the door became clear to the major. It was a black propeller on a yellow background. The major was suddenly hit with the reality of the ramifications what was happening to them both. The major reflected on their scientist's deaths from rather unusual circumstances.

"You may be right. Our top scientists did die under rather unusual circumstances. Or at least that's what the official country newspaper reported."

"I bet you they all died of radiation poisoning, like we are."

"How long do you think we have, Michael?"

"I don't know. Weeks, maybe only a few days. But, I want aboard that ship to look around."

"Why, that ship is an old rust bucket."

"For an old rust bucket, that ship is sitting pretty low in the water like there is some sort of heavy cargo aboard."

"I'll see what I can do. Now, please let me get some sleep."

Michael let the major go back to sleep. As he was returning to his room, another tooth fell out as he was dozing off.

# Chapter 6

The *USS Grand Junction* was once again pier side at the Norfolk Naval Base. After the repairs were completed, the ship did another set of sea and shock trials. This time, no damage was noted and the ship was released to the active duty side of the U.S. Navy. This morning, as the morning sun was burning off the fog, the ship was silent.

The captain woke up early, did his exercises and ate his breakfast in his stateroom. The morning message traffic had arrived and was in the process of being decoded. The radioman first class petty officer in the radio room handed the executive officer a priority message for the captain.

The executive officer pulled out his reading glasses from his right shirt pocket and put them on to read the message. After he read the message, he shook his head in total disbelief. He handed the message back to the radioman first class who stared back at the executive officer strangely.

"This message is a joke, right?" said the executive officer.

"No, sir, not that I know of and if it is a joke, then it came from our boss," replied the radioman first class.

"Decode this message again, would you?"

"Yes, sir."

A few minutes later, the message had been decoded a second and even a third time to make sure that the message was in the right format and the right decoding process had been used. The executive officer read the message again and looked at the radioman first class.

"RM1, has there been anything in the news about us going to war?"

"No, sir, not a word."

"Okay. You are hereby ordered not to discuss this message with anyone except the captain and myself. I'll take this message to the captain."

"Yes, sir."

The executive officer left and made his way to the captain's stateroom. He knocked and then entered. The captain was just putting on his uniform and placing his rank on the lapels when the executive officer walked into the stateroom. The captain went over to his dining table and picked up his cup of coffee and started to drink it.

"Good morning, XO, how are we doing?" asked the captain nonchalantly.

"I think we might be going to war with someone soon," he said.

"Oh, what gives you that idea?" he asked, lowering his cup of coffee.

"This message, skipper," replied the executive officer, handing the message to the captain.

The captain took the message and read it. He shook his head a little in disbelief and set the message down on the tabletop. The captain looked back at the executive officer and pursed his lips together before he spoke.

"I can understand, XO, from this message's content, that you would think we were going to war. However, were there any other messages to tell us where to go or who to challenge?"

"No, sir, not yet."

"Were there any messages received that were giving us direct orders to do any type of combat activity?"

"No, sir. I'm sorry for over reacting to this message."

"That's okay, that's why I chose you to be my executive officer. How much of the crew is aboard right now?"

"About 60 percent."

"This message, since no other messages followed giving specific instructions to us, may be a test of some kind. The Navy will sometimes periodically do that to test and see if the commanding officer will do what he is told. For now, we will follow the orders outlined in this message. Call the department heads and ask them to recall all their personnel."

"Yes, sir."

"Once that is done, notify the Norfolk Naval Base harbor master that I need to get underway by 0915 hours."

"Yes, sir; anything else?"

"Have the navigator report to me immediately. This message instructs me to go to the Yorktown Naval Weapons Station for partial on load. From there, we are to go to Naval Weapons Station, Earl, New Jersey for the rest of the on load."

"Yes, sir, it will be done."

"How many other people know about this message?"

"Only you, me and the radioman first class petty officer that decoded the message this morning."

"Good, the less that know, the better, dismissed XO."

The executive officer left and the captain was left wondering what was really going on. The captain knew that once the missiles were aboard, that he had to get underway as soon as possible to get his main armament. From there, he would take on supplies at sea and go to wherever Admiral Atwell commanded him to go. For the captain, the lone message troubled him greatly. His first instinct was to reach for the cell phone and call Admiral Atwell directly, but he decided against that.

He put the cell phone down and went about getting the ship ready to get underway in less than two hours.

The ship was readied to get underway. The crew did their various jobs and the ship was pulled out into the harbor. Once the ship was clear of the pier, she was assisted no further by the tugs. The trip seemed like a long one, but it was relatively short.

The ship was moored pier side a few hours later at the Yorktown Naval Weapons Station. As a precaution, the port side anchor was dropped into the water to help hold the ship against the pier from the force of the James River trying to push it out to sea. Once the ship was anchored, the sea and anchor detail was secured.

Within minutes of being tied up to the pier, trucks started to roll onto the pier. The crane operator went to work as well. The first things loaded were the HARPOON anti-ship missiles. Next the TOMAHAWKS, both anti-ship and land assault types, were loaded. Finally a dual on load for the Anti-Submarine Rockets and torpedoes commenced. This evolution took all day and wasn't completed until dusk.

When the final part of the weapons on load was completed, it was nightfall. The pier and ship were now bathed in the light provided by enormous spotlights on the pier. It was then that the captain decided that it was too risky to get underway at night, opting for first light instead. A few minutes later, before lights out on the ship, around 2150 hours, the captain called the quarterdeck.

"Good evening, Messenger Of the Watch, Seamen Alstairs," he said.

"Yes, Seamen Alstairs, this is the captain. I want you to pass the word for an all officers meeting in the wardroom."

"Yes, sir."

The messenger of the watch hung up the phone. He pressed the ship wide announcement button and a tone sounded throughout the ship. He spoke into the microphone. He looked at the time and decided to make the announcement for the evening prayer as well.

"All officers meeting in the wardroom, all officers meeting in the wardroom. Tatu, Tatu, stand-by for the evening prayer."

The officers, after the evening prayer was said, gathered in the wardroom. All the officers were talking among themselves. Most were not overly concerned, except that some departments were on high alert status for any rumor. As the captain walked down the passageway to the wardroom, he could hear everyone talking. He opened the door and the wardroom became silent. The officers took their seats as the executive officer stood up and shut the door behind the captain, locking it.

"Ladies and Gentlemen, I called this meeting to get a current report on the ship's status and to let you know what is going on," said the captain.

He paused before continuing.

"Weapons officer, status?"

"We are now fully loaded out with missiles, torpedoes and rockets. We have been further supplied with more flare and chaff charges as well."

"Are all the vertical launch and torpedo tubes loaded?"

"Yes, sir and my crew are ready for anything. However, we still don't have main armament."

"You'll have what you need in 72 to 96 hours; Navigator."

"Yes, sir?" he responded.

"When can we get underway?"

"First light, about 0545 hours."

"Be prepared to get underway at first light and plot me a speed course up the eastern seaboard to Naval Weapons Station, Earl, New Jersey."

"Yes, sir."

"Supply Officer, I have received instructions that we are to be fully loaded out with supplies by the time we leave Earl, New Jersey. You are hereby further instructed to submit your supply list directly to the Supply Officer of Naval Weapons Station, Earl, New Jersey."

"Yes, sir."

"Chief Engineer and Reactor Officer, I want the ship to be ready to get underway at first light. Set your respective sea and anchor details at 0445 hours."

"Yes, sir," they responded.

"Now, here is the official word. Early this morning, I received a message from Admiral Atwell. His instructions to this ship were, take on full combat load. Once we leave Earl, New Jersey, further instructions will follow. I'm thinking this may be a test of some kind, since no other messages followed this one. If this is not a test, then we are about to go kick some poor country's ass. Now, let's get some sleep; dismissed."

Everybody left the wardroom. The captain knew it would was going to be a short night. The night did end very quickly, for the captain and the crew it seemed like they just went to sleep when first light arrived. The ship set the sea and anchor detail at 0500 hours. The anchor was brought aboard as the sun was trying to chase away the night; gray rain clouds were hanging over the Yorktown Naval Weapons Station.

As the ship passed by the piers at the Norfolk Naval Base, the clouds hid the ships further down than piers 11 and 12. The captain watched as the first of two tunnels he had to pass over disappeared under the ship's propellers. About 40 minutes later, the second tunnel disappeared under the ship's propellers. The captain increased the speed a little now that they had passed over the tunnels. Once the ship had cleared Chesapeake Lighthouse, the captain set his bow in the direction of Naval Weapons Station, Earl, New Jersey, at flank speed; the ship was holding 38 knots.

Meanwhile, the captain of the cargo carrier returned from his meeting with the new Libyan President. He was briefing his crew as to what was needed to get done. The ship, by Presidential Order had to get underway within the next 48 hours. The crew responded that they would be ready as the captain finished off the briefing with the final word as to what the mission of this armor plated cargo carrier really was. They were to sail to within 300 nautical miles of the U.S. east coast and launch all the Al-Fatah II series missiles. He went on to explain that the ship would be set to autopilot once they cleared the Strait of Gibraltar.

Michael and the major were swimming towards the ship slowly so as to not be detected by a topside sentry. They were also swimming slowly because of their extreme fatigue from the radiation sickness. When they arrived at the outboard side of the ship, Michael tapped the hull with his hand and it sounded very odd. He looked at the major who also tapped the hull. Then they both tapped the hull as they floated together.

"That hull has the appearance of being more solid than I thought," said the major.

"Yes, it is. In fact, it feels almost like armor plating," replied Michael hoarsely.

"Armor plating? What would an old cargo carrier need armor plating for?"

"I don't know, but there seems to be a lot of activity on the ship now."

"Yes, there does seem to be a lot more activity. I still don't know why a civilian cargo carrier needs armor plating."

"I don't have an answer for that either. I'm really curious to know what her cargo is."

"In the morning, we can look at her cargo manifest."

"Sounds good."

Michael and the major swam slowly back to shore. Once they were on shore, they stepped into the major's vehicle and drove to his house. The next day, the major and Michael were able to look at the cargo manifest. They discovered that the cargo carrier's manifest listed the cargo aboard as classified. The major asked the captain to see inside the cargo holds, but the captain refused. The captain went on to state that a special Presidential Order sealed the cargo aboard. Michael and the major were dumbfounded, but the major was determined to find out what was aboard the ship.

That night, Michael took out one of his Palm Pilot® devices and turned it on. Located at the end of the stylus, which was really a metal probe, was a small patch of wires in a square shape sticker to detect other things including radiation. That night, Michael and the major slipped aboard the ship. They climbed slowly and breathing heavily up the hawse pipe. The hawse pipe, which was located on the bow of the ship, was where the anchor chain and the anchor fit. Once aboard the ship, Michael pulled out his Palm Pilot® device and started sampling the ship. When they were done, they crawled back down the anchor chain via the hawse pipe and swam to shore.

They drove back to the major's house where, after a long sleep, Michael turned on his Palm Pilot® device and waited for the results. When the Palm Pilot® started beeping, Michael and the major went down into the major's bunker to view the results. Michael used the major's computer with a secure line on it, to download the device and a few seconds later the results appeared on the computer screen. The results were not what the Michael or the major were expecting. Michael had the computer print up the results as well.

The results showed that the ship was indeed armor plated with a six-inch thick outer hull. The computer identified the armor plate as "HY-110, Class 'A' armor plating found primarily on warships and tanks." The next sets of results were even more puzzling; the cargo hatches, which Michael and the major were expecting to be made of steel, were not. The hatches were four-inch thick, solid lead sheets with Hafnium and Zirconium laminates on the tops and bottoms. The final sets of results were astounding.

"Detectable levels of radioactivity are present. Particles of Gamma and X-rays detectable at low levels. The bottom plates of the cargo hold, from echo sounding, are made of a specialized steel used primarily in blast deflector plating for launching rockets and missiles." Michael turned to the major.

"Major, why does a cargo carrier need to be outfitted with blast deflector plating and solid cargo hatches made with lead and Hafnium and Zirconium laminates?"

"I don't know."

Michael figured out why the ship had all that extra equipment and plating aboard; the ship was going to be used as a Trojan Horse to attack another country.

"Major, I think your country has nuclear weapons," said Michael.

"I never thought it was possible; how?"

"I'm going to guess that some of your scientists figured out that your reactors could make small enough amounts of weapons grade Plutonium so as to not be noticed by either the International Atomic Energy Association or the U.N. Weapons Inspectors."

"But why? For what purpose could my country have for creating nuclear weapons?"

"Attack the United States with a quick strike to slow up its response time to a threat that could not be easily detected. Using a civilian cargo carrier to launch the attack was a very wise thing to do. Think about it major, do you really think that the U.S. Navy would fire on a civilian ship?"

"Probably not. It is a well conceived plan, I must admit that."

"I think I know now where those Al-Fatah II series missiles are at; aboard that ship in the cargo holds already in an upright position ready to fire. You've got to warn someone right away."

"I will."

# Chapter 7

The morning sun was rising on New York City. The sunlight was soon reflecting off the glass of the buildings to the streets below. Another day was beginning for the United Nations ambassadors. The U.S. ambassador to the United Nations was completing up some paperwork. After having some coffee and viewing an Internet website on missiles of the world, he walked across the hall to see if the ambassador for Mexico was in his office. The Mexican Ambassador was in his office. The U.S. ambassador knocked on his office door and then entered.

"Good morning, Ambassador Felix, can I have a word with you?" asked the U.S. ambassador.

"What is on your mind, señor?"

"I received a phone call from a very upset State Department person who wanted me to find out why your country purchased two Al-Fatah II series missiles."

"What is this missile you speak of?"

"Well, from the information I obtained from the Internet, this missile is classified as an intermediate range ballistic missile. It has a range of between 1,100 to 1,300 nautical miles and carries a 2,000 kilogram payload consisting of a high explosive, reverse cone-shaped charge."

"I don't know why my country would purchase such a thing. However, I will call my government and find out, Señor."

"Thanks and when you find out, please call me and we will see if a deal can be worked out; perhaps some of those medical supplies, equipment and trainers."

"I think something can be arranged, Señor."

The ambassador's next stop was to see the Ecuadorian Ambassador, Hector Alvarez. The American Ambassador asked the same question and received the same answer; I don't know. However, the Ecuadorian Ambassador decided to make the phone call directly. As it turned out, the Ecuadorian Army had never purchased the missiles. Hector thought that maybe the information the American Ambassador had was faulty. The American Ambassador thanked Hector for his time and returned to his office.

Meanwhile the information was received in Bill's desk. Bill looked at it and merely made sure that the CIA and the Department of Homeland Security were also given the information. Bill headed off to another meeting; only this meeting was with Becky Strohmetz. Bill wanted to make the funeral arrangements for Michael. Becky looked at Bill as they put the final touches on the funeral itself. Bill told Becky he would do everything he could to bring Michael's body home.

As the day progressed, the Mexican ambassador obtained the information. He wrote down the particulars and thanked his President for his helpfulness in the matter. The Mexican President requested that the medical supplies, equipment and trainers be expedited if possible. As the ambassador hung up the phone, half a world away, a ship was getting ready to set sail for the United States. The phone rang in the U.S. ambassador's office.

"Hello?" asked the U.S. ambassador.

"Señor, I have your information. Before I give it to you, my country's President has a request."

"What is it that your President wants?" He already knew the answer.

"He wants the promised medical supplies, equipment and trainers."

"I will expedite the request and you can call a news conference to announce the big news of a state-of-the-art hospital in Mexico City."

"Fair enough, Señor, you have proven good to your word so far."

"And I will continue being fair into the future. Now, about that information."

"Señor, my government told me it purchased those two missiles to be put on display in our Militaries of the World Theme Park in Mexico City."

"So, what you're saying is, they are merely museum pieces?"

"Yes, Señor."

"Thank you and I will see to it that the medical supplies, equipment and trainers are flown into Mexico City in the next, say, 96 hours and without any major government hassles, okay?"

"Fair enough, Señor, have a good day."

"You too."

The U.S. ambassador hung up the phone. He then picked up the phone and called Bill Yancy at the State Department. The secretary who answered the phone was nice enough to pull Bill out of a meeting for this call.

"Bill, here," said Mr. Yancy.

"Mr. Yancy, I was able to obtain the answer to your question that you asked me. According to the Mexican ambassador, the missiles were purchased to be used as museum pieces in some sort of Militaries of the World Theme Park, in Mexico City."

"Thank you, I appreciate that information and I would like to say I'm sorry for our first meeting on the telephone; I was a little stressed out."

"I understand and you have a good day."

"You too."

They both hung up the phone at the same time. Bill went back to his meeting and the ambassador went about making good on his promise. Now, at CIA headquarters and within the Department of Homeland Security, the information was being processed and analyzed. Almost instantly, a problem was found in the information about the cargo ship; the fax was incomplete.

The information was processed anyway and then filed for future reference. The Department of Homeland Security, however, was trying to deal with a new problem. This new problem took people away from the Libyan affair and placed them on this one. The Secretary of Homeland Security was reviewing a report he had received from the Department of Transportation Secretary. The Secretary of Transportation decided that a total news blackout was best and allowed no communication either to or from the stricken Coast Guard Cutter. After reviewing the report, the Secretary of Homeland Security picked up the phone and called the White House.

"Good morning, this is the White House, how can I help you?" said the voice.

"Yes, this is the Secretary of Homeland Security. Code clearance Blue, please put me through to the President of the United States, this is very urgent."

"Yes, sir, Mr. Secretary, I will put you right through."

There was a pause before the President picked up the phone.

"Hello, Homeland Security, what can I do for you?" asked the President.

"Sir, are we on a secure line?"

"One moment," said the President, switching the phone call to the orange colored phone on his desk in the Oval Office.

"What's going on?" asked the President.

"Two days ago, according to the report I have in front of me, a group of pirates attacked a Coast Guard Cutter that was on routine patrol in the area."

"Were there any casualties?"

"Seven killed, one classified as Missing in Action."

"How much damage?"

"Mostly the superstructure starboard side from bow to amidships. There was some damage inflicted aft. The hull was punctured in two places by some sort of weapon the captain called a chain-gun. Several 30mm fragments were recovered."

"Where's the ship now?"

"The ship is pier side at a repair facility in Key West, Florida. It was the only place the ship could make it to without drawing unnecessary attention to itself. The Secretary of Transportation has cut off all communications until I give him the okay to restore them."

"Good plan, he's a smart man, that Transportation Secretary. What is the estimated downtime?"

"The ship is an older Coast Guard Cutter and was scheduled for a service life extension program. The estimated downtime is three to five months."

"Any theories as to why the pirates attacked a Coast Guard Cutter?"

"The captain of the Coast Guard Cutter, due to its smaller size, thinks the pirates mistook him for a private yacht that was on their scopes in the area. They were attacked and the Coast Guard Cutter returned fire. He also reports that during the attack a prototype dye marker shell and something called a Mark-179, Magnetic Tracking Device were used."

"In other words, we marked them. That was very resourceful thinking of the person or persons who came up with that plan. I'll call the Chief of Naval Operations. Your instructions are to maintain communications blackout until further notice."

"Yes, sir."

The President hung up the phone and placed a call to the Chief of Naval Operations office. The secretary who answered the phone said that Admiral Nagomu was in the bathroom. The President said he would wait.

"Good morning, sir. What can I do for you?" asked Admiral Nagomu.

"Well, a good morning to you to Admiral Nagomu. Yes, there is something that you can do for me."

"What is that, sir?"

"We have a goddamn problem in the Caribbean and I want you to personally take care of the problem."

"What sort of problem in the Caribbean, sir?" asked the admiral, starting to take notes.

"It seems that some pirates down there attacked a Coast Guard Cutter mistaking it for a private yacht in the area of the same size. I'm considering going to threat level Orange, but I will let you know."

"What sort of problem fixing did you want me to do, sir?"

"I want you to send something big into the Caribbean. I don't want some sort of small ship like a destroyer or frigate because it might get mistaken for a private yacht. I want something big."

"I'm sorry, sir, we no longer have the battleships and most of my navy on the eastern seaboard is in the shipyards undergoing service life extension programs."

"Can you do the job?"

"Yes, sir. What are your guidelines?"

"Whoop those pirates' ass. Show them the United States is a force to be reckoned with. If they surrender, fine, if not, give them everything you've got."

"Yes, sir."

"By the way, some clever individuals used a dye marker and something called a Mark-179 something or another. I think those people should get some sort of an award or medal of some kind."

"Yes, sir. I think something can be arranged."

"Don't fail me, admiral. Good-bye."

The President hung up the phone at the same time the Chief of Naval Operations did. The Chief of Naval Operations thumbed through his phone book on his desktop to find the number for the Commander-in-Chief of Atlantic Fleet Forces. He dialed the first number listed as the admiral's office. Admiral Nagomu found out that Admiral Jamison was not in the office. Admiral Nagomu then looked down the list and located Admiral Jamison's cell phone. Admiral Nagomu dialed that number and Admiral Jamison answered the phone.

"Commander-in-Chief Atlantic Fleet Forces, Admiral Jamison speaking," he said.

"Admiral Jamison, this Admiral Nagomu. The President called me about a problem he wants fixed in a big way. In fact, our Commander-in-Chief said to me, and I quote, 'Whoop those pirates' ass. If they surrender, fine, if not, give them everything we have got.' Did you get all of that, admiral?"

"Yes, sir, I certainly did," replied the admiral, writing down notes on a notepad that was on his desktop. "Was there anything else, sir?"

"Yes, he said, 'I want something big in the Caribbean. I don't want a destroyer or frigate mistaken for a private yacht.' Did you get that?"

"Yes, sir. Seems logical to me. Let me see what I have available."

"He wants it done soon, admiral. You will call me back when you have something ready?"

"Yes, sir."

The line went dead as the President prepared for an emergency press conference. He stepped up onto the stage and stood at the podium and arranged his notes for the press conference. He motioned for silence before reading the prepared speech.

"Ladies and Gentlemen of the Press. There has been an incident in the Caribbean involving some pirates and a Coast Guard Cutter. The military theory is, the pirates, who may have been tracking a private yacht in the vicinity of the Coast Guard Cutter, mistook the Cutter for the yacht. During the altercation, the Coast Guard Cutter sustained heavy damage to the superstructure and the loss of some lives. At this time, I am raising the country's threat level to Orange until the heartless attack by these cowards is resolved. Your government will not stand for this type of attack, nor will it let this attack go unpunished; that is all."

The President left the podium without answering any questions. On the way back to one of his other meetings, he called the Secretary of Homeland Security to inform him of the decision to raise the threat level to Orange. This decision was based upon the seriousness of the attack on the Coast Guard Cutter. The press soon released the President's statement. The news blackout was now over for the ship and the crew. Now, all the President could do was wait and see what kind of plan the Chief of Naval Operations had come up with.

Meanwhile, the *USS Grand Junction* was pulling pier side at Naval Weapons Station, Earl, New Jersey, for her on load of main armament. The ship was to be fully loaded out in two days. After the ship was loaded up and provisioned out, the ship was to be put back to sea to receive further orders.  Currently, the ship was still pier side at the weapons station.

The Commander-in-chief of Atlantic Fleet Forces was reviewing his ship listing and status. Most of his fleet was either in the shipyards or in dry-dock undergoing major repairs or service life extension programs. As he looked over the list, he came to the page that listed the new ships of the fleet. The newest name was CA-144, *USS Grand Junction.*

Admiral Jamison looked at the ship's status and classification. The ship's status was full active duty and the ship's classification was "Heavy Cruiser." The ship had been recently promoted to the "Active Duty" phase from "Pre-Commissioning" phase only four days ago. He looked at the ship's current location; Naval Weapons Station, Earl, New Jersey, for load out. He then looked at the place where the ship needed to be.

The distance was 5,000 nautical miles. The ship could be there in five days at flank speed. The admiral turned around to face his computer in his office and called up a blank message to be filled in. He typed the message, which was four pages long, and sent it off coded and labeled it priority.

The message was received and decoded. It was almost nightfall in New Jersey. The ship had finally received the last of the supplies that the Supply Officer had requested. The ship was now over 10 feet lower in the water and several thousand tons heavier. The Supply Officer was the Officer of the Deck when the last of the supplies arrived on the pier to be loaded aboard. The duty radioman received and decoded the message. Once the message had been decoded, the radioman called the quarterdeck.

"Quarterdeck, Quartermaster First Class Johnson speaking, how may I help you?" he said.

"Yes, this is Radioman First Class Alvarez in the radio room, can I speak to the Officer of the Deck?"

"One moment," said Johnson as he handed the phone over to the Supply Officer.

"Officer of the Deck, Commander Milligan," he said.

"Yes, sir. I have a priority message with restricted delivery to the captain in the radio room."

"I'll be right up to get it."

"Yes, sir."

The Supply Officer hung up the phone and headed towards the radio room. Along the way, he stopped to look at the flags flying from the flag bridge. There were no flags flying to indicate that the commanding officer was not aboard. The Supply Officer took the message and proceeded to the captain's stateroom. He knocked on the captain's stateroom door before entering.

"Good evening, skipper. I have a priority message with restricted delivery to you, sir," said the Supply Officer, handing the captain the clipboard that the message was attached to.

The captain stood up from his desk and took the clipboard. He opened up the clipboard cover and started reading the four-page message. The orders were from the Chief of Naval Operations via the Commander-in-Chief of Atlantic Fleet Forces. There was no one listed on the information line of the message. The captain, after reading the message completely one more time, closed the clipboard and looked at the Supply Officer.

"Did you read this message?" asked the captain.

"No, sir, I don't get that nosey. If it is important, then I figure you will tell us," replied the Supply Officer.

"You're right. Please pass the word to set the sea and anchor detail at first light. Once we are secured from the sea and anchor detail, inform the department heads to meet with me in the wardroom."

"Aye, sir."

"Dismissed."

It was another short night and even a longer day. The ship was underway at 0600 hours. The sea and anchor detail was secured at 1200 hours. Shortly after that, the captain briefed the department heads. Stepping out onto the bridge, the captain barked the next set of orders.

"Attention on the bridge, I have the conn," said the captain.

The captain walked over to his chair that was on the bridge and looked up at the phone above it. He grabbed the receiver and turned the selector switch to Navigation.

"Bridge, Navigation," said the captain.

"Navigation, aye," replied the navigator.

"Set your course for the Caribbean."

"Aye, sir."

The captain put the receiver back up into its cradle and turned to face the helmsman and lee helmsman.

"Lee helm, set your speed to flank."

"Aye, sir, flank speed."

The ship lunged forward, taking on the ocean with confidence.

# Chapter 8

The Libyan registered ship was being loaded up with fuel and provisions. Fuel trucks were lined up on the pier as far back as the gate and onto the access road. Provisions of all sorts were arriving as well. Michael and the major were watching from a hillside that overlooked the Tripoli bay area. They set their binoculars down as the sun rose higher and higher into the sky. Even with the vehicle's air-conditioning on, the heat of the desert day could be felt inside. Michael and the major both knew that time for them was getting short, maybe only days now. They had no hair on their heads and all but three teeth had fallen out of Michael's mouth. The major had already lost all of his teeth. They picked up their binoculars again as Michael spoke hoarsely.

"What do you think they are doing?" asked Michael, very hoarsely.

"I would say, with all those trucks lined up on the pier, getting ready to set sail would be my guess," replied the major through his lips, which were being pulled into his mouth from lack of teeth.

"Mine too. Since we have so little time left, let's try and get aboard that ship tonight. We need to find out what her cargo really is and where she really is going."

"Good idea."

That night, weak and very fatigued, Michael and the major climbed up a mooring line. Once they were aboard, they found the first place they could find to rest. After resting for a little while, they moved around the ship. They were careful to be ever alert for the ship's crew; if they spotted the ship's crew, they would find cover in the area they were in. Finally, they both made it to the forward cargo hold area.

The doors at both ends of the passageway they were in were welded shut. They went to the other side and found those doors welded shut as well. As they were trying to move towards the amidships cargo hold, they heard someone coming down the ladder towards their position. The major looked around and located a small maintenance shop. The major found the door was open; quickly they both ducked into it, closing the door behind them.

When the person had left, Michael fumbled around inside the maintenance shop and located a flashlight. The flashlight's batteries were weak, but it still shone some light. Slowly, the major opened the door a crack to see if anyone was standing outside. Looking up and down the passageway to make sure that no one was coming, Michael and the major started to look around again. They walked around both port and starboard sides of the amidships cargo hold. Both of the doors on the aft end were welded shut, however, Michael found that the starboard side cargo hold access door was not welded shut.

The major stood lookout while Michael used all of his strength to open the door. Michael thought the door was heavy and when he opened it, the light from the passageway showed that the door had blast deflector plating attached to it. As Michael shined his flashlight around the cargo hold, he found the entire deck was made of this blast deflector plating. He cautiously moved inside the cargo hold and tripped over something. Shining his flashlight in the general direction of where he tripped, his flashlight illuminated a fin.

Michael's weak flashlight beam lit up the fin to where it connected with the fuselage. He shone his weak beam of light up as far as it could go. It was an Al-Fatah II series missile, upright and ready for launch. The major stepped into the cargo hold with Michael and looked at what Michael had found. Michael finally raised himself off the deck and shined his flashlight up and down the missile.

"Oh my God, this is an Al-Fatah II series missile and it looks ready for launch," said the major.

"This whole cargo hold and the ones forward and aft of this one are probably full of them, major."

"How many do you think?"

"Probably all of them that were unaccounted for that I was told about during my mission briefing."

"Then if these cargo holds are full of missiles, then my country is planning an attack of some kind. Surmising that these are the missiles that are unaccounted for, then they may have those tactical nuclear warheads attached."

"Who is your country going to attack?" asked Michael.

"Maybe the United States is their target. You said it yourself only a few hours ago."

"Then we must warn the United States of this impending attack. Even if it turns out to be a hoax."

"But how, even if we could, what would we tell them? With our current information we have, it's really sketchy."

"That's a good point. Then I suggest that we find out what those missiles' intended targets really are."

"Good plan, maybe they left something around here."

The major and Michael searched all night long without finding anything. Tired and exhausted, they found a place to rest inside the access door to a maintenance shop fan room. It was noisy in the fan room, but comfortable and out of the way. When they had slept for some time, the fan room went silent. Michael noticed, as he opened his right eye to look around, that the lights flickered a little and then the fan stopped and started back up. As Michael was about to doze off again, he heard voices coming from down below him. He moved to the edge of the fan's enormous fan screen to listen in on their conversation.

"The captain wants to get underway, how soon?" asked one voice.

"We can get underway in 24 hours. Tell the captain that I must have a stable plant for at least that long since the boilers haven't been used in 10 years."

"I will let the captain know that engineer. But why do we have to wait 24 hours?"

"With the boilers having been in lay up for so long, I need the 24 hours to make sure that we don't drop fires somewhere out at sea."

"Very well, I will let the captain know."

The conversation ended and that is when Michael knew he and the major were the only thing standing between the Libyans and a nuclear attack on the United States. Michael went back to sleep and woke up when he heard the fan room door open. Michael looked to see who it was who had entered the fan room.

The major was returning from a food gathering and scouting expedition. The major had appropriated some soft foods for them to eat. They ate the food praying that with every bite that the food would stay down. Now, both men had lost their teeth. The major was starting to have blood showing up in his urine. Michael was doing a little better, but he knew that the end was coming soon. That night, he and the major wandered around the ship again. This time, they headed towards the bridge and chart room.

When they arrived on the bridge, they checked carefully for signs that it was inhabited. Finding no one on the bridge, they looked around for anything that would give them more clues as to what the ship really had in her cargo holds and where the ship was going. Michael realized, as he looked at the clock on the bridge, which was displaying local time, that he was probably presumed dead. He remembered that regulations were specific; Chapter 110, Section 104, Paragraph C, which read, "If contact has been lost or no contact has been reestablished in 96 hours, consider the operative captured, dead or…."

When he and the major were done with the bridge, they moved to the chart room. When they entered the chart room, they started searching there. Michael came across some unusually accurate charts. The charts were of the eastern seaboard of the United States. The charts covered the east coast of Florida, the east coast of Georgia and the east coast of South Carolina. There were charts of the Gulf of Mexico states as well. The gulf coast states of Alabama and Mississippi were shown in amazing detail. Michael was about to put the maps up, when he saw a faint red line on one of them.

Opening up the chart further, Michael noticed that the red line marked an old shipping route that wasn't used all that much. From this red line were purple lines going outward to points on the other maps. Looking at the major to see if the coast was clear, Michael moved the charts closer to the tiny, bright white lamp that was still turned on located at the far end of the chart table. He set the charts out and matched the purple lines up with the other maps. What he discovered horrified him. The Libyans were definitely planning an attack against the United States.

From the red line, which would put the ship about 400 nautical miles offshore at the furthest point, to the closest point, 315 nautical miles, to where the purple lines ended on land, showed Michael something he would never forget. The purple lines were the intended flight paths for the Al-Fatah II series missiles. The missiles were to be launched at different targets at different times. On the purple lines were the estimated flight times to those cities targeted.

The cities targeted, marked with orange stars on the maps, included Miami, Orlando, and Tampa Bay, Florida. Atlanta and Kings Bay, Georgia were targeted as well. Charleston and Columbia, South Carolina were targets along with the Gulf Coast states.

Pensacola, Florida, Pascagoula, Mississippi, Birmingham, Alabama were intended targets. For those missiles fired closer to shore, the interior cities of Biloxi, Mississippi and Mobile Bay, Alabama. Further inside the United States, cities in the states of Virginia, North Carolina and Tennessee were plotted as well. Michael knew, by counting the number of intended cities that the numbers of missiles were probably equal to or greater than the number of targets.

The maps also showed other missile attack cities as well. Those other cities showed up on the maps as gray lines. Those other cities included Cape Canaveral, Key West and Ft. Lauderdale, Florida. Other attacks were going to be carried out against National Forests, Parks and Historical Sites. As Michael put up the charts back into their holes in the chart room, the major tapped Michael on the left shoulder. Michael turned around to see the major holding a large, three-ring notebook binder filled with numbers. Michael read the numbers and noticed that the names of the targets were in direct proportion to the missile targets. The major spoke to Michael hoarsely.

"Michael, these numbers, which are directly across from the name of the city or place to be missile attacked, seems to indicate the possible amount of civilian casualties from the attack. I think the red numbers are for the initial attack and the blue numbers are for after the attack, possibly."

Michael briefly reviewed the numbers and shook his head in acknowledgement to this person's understanding of a military formula called LD5030.

"Someone in your military, major, understands the formula of LD5030."

"LD5030? What is this LD5030 formula?" asked the major.

"LD5030 is a military formula that you can use to calculate the loss of personnel, in this case civilians, with the use of a nuclear, chemical or biological weapon. It would appear that someone estimated the loss of civilians. In this case, LD5030 is where 50 percent of the civilians will die in the first 30 days after the initial attack with those nuclear warheads."

"I'm so sorry, Michael, that my country plans on doing this senseless act against your country."

"We will deal with that issue later. Right now, make sure we put everything back up into the right spots. I don't want anyone suspecting that there are stowaways aboard."

"Okay, besides, I'm getting tired."

"It is almost sunrise. Let's get out of here and get some sleep."

Michael and the major put back everything that they had taken out. The major managed to appropriate some more soft food for them and they ate. Once again they prayed that the food would stay down. The food did stay down and they soon fell asleep. Before they both were fully awake, they felt a large bump that shuddered the ship from one end to the other. Since they rotated fan rooms, this fan room was located forward up by the chain locker for the anchor chain. The major looked at Michael and they strained their ears to hear what the voices were saying just outside the fan room. They heard some shouting and then the anchor was raised up. The links of the anchor chain bumped and banged as the chain came aboard. Michael and the major held their breath.

The fan in the fan room stopped running briefly as the light went out completely this time. The bumping and banging of the anchor chain going into the chain locker soon stopped and several more shudders were felt the entire length of the ship. They both listened closely as the ship's horn sounded several blasts. As this happened, Michael and the major felt movement of the ship. The ship and its lethal cargo were now underway. Michael looked at the major as the lights came back on again.

"Major, I realize that neither one of us is very strong anymore. But, we must stop this ship from reaching the east coast of the United States at all costs," Michael said hoarsely.

"I don't think we can stop this ship," replied the major, just as hoarsely.

"Why not?"

"Just before we set sail, I had to go to the bathroom. I noticed that there are armed guards outside the radio room, the entrances to both the boiler and engine rooms and outside the galley and food storage areas."

"Then we must have been sloppy and left something behind or out of place that gave us away."

"Perhaps we didn't get a chart in the right place or maybe the missing food gave us away. Michael I was very careful about getting our food," said the major.

"Could be that maybe the captain expected some of the crew to mutiny when the captain announced his diabolical plans to the crew. But, since we cannot stop this ship, we must find some way of warning the U.S. military about this ship and Libya's plans."

"How, I told you that the radio room is heavily guarded with several armed guards."

"I know. I'm thinking right now. Our best bet now is to wait, what I estimate to be 36 hours, for the ship to be into the Atlantic."

"What happens then?"

"We jump over the side of the ship with a life raft. I still have my emergency locator beacon on me. I'll write down the message that needs to be transmitted to the U.S. military authorities. When we pass away and our bodies are found, hopefully the message will get to the right people in time."

"That sounds like a good plan. The life raft does have provisions for a few days," said the major.

The ship continued on its course. That night, when Michael and the major stepped out into the night air, Michael estimated the ship's speed to be a constant 18 knots. He scribbled down a note on some discarded paper they had found on an earlier expedition. Michael finished off the message with an approximate position based on the compass built into the major's watch.

The next morning found the ship approaching the Strait of Gibraltar. Michael and the major counted their hours before they jumped ship. Before they jumped ship, Michael had the major locate a container that could be sealed. Michael placed the message into the container and closed the lid up tight.

As night began to fall, Michael and the major said their prayers to their respective deities and grabbed the life raft from a locker that was not locked up or guarded heavily. With message firmly attached to him and the other hand on the life raft, he jumped. The major jumped with him and they hit the water hard from the deck of the ship being, Michael estimated, some seven meters to the water.

The ship disappeared into the night as the life raft inflated and came to an upright position. Once they had crawled inside the life raft, Michael pulled out his emergency locator beacon and turned it on. Although the red LED light didn't come on, Michael thought it was transmitting, but it wasn't. They now waited for death to come to them, for both of them were tired of suffering.

As the sun started to rise, Michael looked at the major. His eyes were wide open and staring, blankly, into the morning sky. Michael waved his right hand over the major's eyes to check for any type of reaction. The pupils of the eyes were not reacting in any way to the waving of Michael's hand. Next, Michael reached down the major's left arm to feel for a pulse. He couldn't find a pulse either. Slowly, he used his right hand to close the major's eyes. The sun was warming things up and Michael finally dozed off after saying good-bye to the major. While he fitfully dozed in the life raft, he entered a most wonderful dream state.

He was looking at flowers and trees with absolutely brilliant colors. There was a slight breeze blowing and to Michael it felt warm and comforting; almost soothing to him. As he looked around this field, he started to see many familiar faces. One of those faces was Gilda Hanson's. She stepped forward and touched Michael's left hand. He looked into her face and smiled.

"Isn't this place wonderful, Michael?" she said.

"Yes, I feel very comfortable and peaceful. What is this place?"

"This is the place the King of kings has set aside for all of us who believe in him to come to when we are about to die."

"Am I dead?"

"Not yet, but I suspect your pain and suffering will be over shortly. Let's go see."

Michael blinked his eyes once and he and Gilda were standing on the ocean. As Michael looked down, he was standing on the edge of the life raft. He stared at his own body, which was convulsing and twitching in a feeble attempt to stay alive. The radiation had emaciated his body to the point where he was nothing more than flesh and bones, which were readily seen. He looked back at Gilda who had once more slipped her hand into his.

"The dying is the easy part, it's the leaving that's hard," she said quietly.

"It's my time, isn't it?" asked Michael.

"Yes, your flesh will cease to exist, but your soul will live forever now. You will be whole once again."

As he watched himself die, he wondered what neat things eternity had in store for him. He soon found out as all those familiar faces took him down a long hallway to a set of large double-doors. Everyone motioned for him to open the doors, but he hesitated. Gilda tapped him on the right shoulder. He turned around to face her.

"It's okay, we will see you on the other side," said Gilda, confidently.

"We?" asked Michael, with a strange look on his face.

"Daddy, hurry up, we can't wait for all eternity," said the little voice.

Michael looked down to see a small child.

"Yes, the child is ours. Our unconditional love for each other allowed all this to happen. Now, go on, time is short."

Michael pulled open the double-doors and entered into the bright light. As the others watched him go into the light, the doors shut behind him.

# Chapter 9

The Chief of Naval Operations looked at his calendar. It had been almost three days since his phone call to Admiral Jamison. The President had already called Admiral Nagomu several times over the last three days. Admiral Nagomu kept telling the President that he had heard nothing as of yet, but when he did, the President would be the first one that Admiral Nagomu said he would call. Impatience almost got the better of Admiral Nagomu. As he reached for the phone, to call Admiral Jamison, it rang instead.

"Hello?" asked Admiral Nagomu.

"Yes, sir. I have the Commander-in-Chief of Atlantic Fleet Forces on line four for you," said YN2 Brown.

"Thank you, YN2 Brown. I'll take the call."

"Yes, sir."

She hung up from the line and Admiral Nagomu looked down at his phone and pressed the button marked line four.

"Good morning, Admiral Jamison, so good to hear from you. What is the report?"

"In accordance with your request from our Commander-In-Chief, I have something big on station in the Caribbean. You can let the President know that I have my newest nuclear powered ship in the fleet, the *USS Grand Junction,* on patrol in the requested area."

"What were the ship's orders?"

"I priority messaged her commanding officer and gave him an explicit set of orders. In fact, I ordered her commanding officer to 'whoop ass', if necessary, on those who had attacked such a poor defenseless Coast Guard Cutter."

"Great news and to think I was almost ready to call you and complain."

"Yes, sir. Now, you won't have to. By the way, I called the commanding officer in charge of the 14th Coast Guard District and informed him of the Commander-In-Chief's request for an award of some kind to be given those brave crew members who took the time to mark one of the pirate ships."

"That was outstanding thinking, Admiral Jamison. Thank you very much; good-bye," said Admiral Nagomu.

"Good-bye to you, too, sir and I'm looking forward to our golf game later on this week," replied Admiral Jamison.

Admiral Jamison hung up the phone and looked at the Norfolk Naval Base from his office window. The morning was bright and clear. There came a knock on his door. A moment later, the master chief petty officer in charge of the radio complex entered the admiral's office to deliver the morning message traffic.

Admiral Jamison reviewed the message traffic, initialed off on them and handed the messages back to the master chief. The master chief departed and went about posting all of the messages to the various departments on the naval base.

Admiral Nagomu picked up his phone and called the President. He let the President know that he had instructed Admiral Jamison to put together a 'top notch' military operation in the Caribbean and that's why it took so long to get the response back to the President. The President was more than pleased with the efforts that Admiral Nagomu had come up with so far on this issue. The only thing that Admiral Nagomu could think of at the present time were the governments of the Caribbean. He requested that the President call the respective governments of the Caribbean to let them know of this military operation and to please stand ready to assist in any way that was deemed necessary. The Admiral figured that it would be a 'token of good will.'

The President agreed and said he would be making those phone calls later on this evening. Admiral Nagomu decided that maybe the International Piracy Center should be notified as well. The President gave the admiral permission to make that phone call. The admiral was about to hang up when the President asked some more questions.

"Admiral Nagomu, did Admiral Jamison say what 'big' thing he had on station down there?" asked the President.

"No, sir, he was not specific about the ship type. However, I would venture a guess at either the *USS Grand Junction,* CA-144 or the *USS Avery,* LHD-5."

"Oh, I see. What exactly is the *USS Grand Junction,* admiral?"

"The ship is classified as a heavy cruiser and is the latest edition to the nuclear powered Navy. The ship is Anti-ship, ant-submarine and counter electronic warfare equipped. In fact, sir, the ship has some very intimidating looks."

"What are the ship's intimidating looks?"

"The ship is 258.3 meters long, 83.3 meters wide and 30 meters tall. The ship, with her triple mounted turrets of 8-inch guns, looks like a miniature battleship."

"That ship sounds most impressive. Remind me one of these days and I will visit the ship. In the meantime, keep up the good work."

"Thank you, sir and have a good day."

The admiral hung up the phone as the day began to brighten even more. The emergency locator beacon signal was never picked up by the repeating station in the Azores due to not having a fully charged battery in the transmitter. The sun rose higher on the surface of the ocean as the life raft floated about in the Atlantic. The life raft had two dead bodies inside it, making the life raft a floating tomb. The life raft was at the mercy of the waves and wind.

A yacht passed within a few meters of the life raft. The small crew of the yacht brought the bloating bodies aboard and wrapped them up in large plastic bags. The large plastic bags were used in case the bodies exploded, they wouldn't dump all their insides out all over the inside of the yacht's freezer. The crew put the bodies inside the yacht's large freezer.

The emergency locator beacon had fallen out of Michael's dead hands along with the canister containing the message. The yacht's captain found the canister and opened it up. He removed the message, put his reading glasses on and read the message. After reading the message, the billionaire tossed it along with his glasses on top of the chart table on the bridge of the yacht. The yacht anchored in the Azores a few hours later.

The billionaire turned the bodies over to the American Consulate personnel whom he had contacted earlier when he found the bodies. The consulate personnel took the bodies from the yacht and put them in their freezers. The yacht's owner departed and post mortem examinations were performed. It would be a few hours for the fingerprint results to come back. In the meantime, the fact that someone was running a record check on Michael's fingerprints sent a silent alert fax to Bill's office. Bill reviewed the alert fax and noticed it was sent from the U.S. Consulate in the Azores. Sitting the fax down on his desktop, he called Becky Strohmetz.

"Hello?" she asked.

"Becky, Michael's body has been recovered," said Bill, choking back tears.

"Where is it at?" she asked, almost ready to cry herself.

"I received a silent alert fax that was initiated from the U.S. Consulate in the Azores. They were running Michael's fingerprints."

"I will make the arrangements to retrieve Michael's body. Bill, I'm so sorry."

"Me too," said Bill, hanging up the phone.

Meanwhile, the *USS Grand Junction* had been on station for 30 hours now. In that time, the ship had stopped several yachts, one powerboat and a speedboat. So far, the only thing that the boarding crews had found was one marijuana cigarette located in the crack of the seat of the speedboat. No other vessels were coming up on the radarscopes. The captain was beginning to wonder if this "hot mission of law enforcement duty" was just a joke. As the day wore on into the night, the captain was about to turn the bridge over to the operations officer when the call box on the bridge came to life.

"Combat, bridge," said the voice.

"Bridge, aye," responded the captain.

"New contact, sir. Contact has been designated Sierra, Charlie fourteen. Bearing 109, speed 12 knots. Electronic Counter Warfare has positively identified her as a freighter."

"Bridge, aye. Distance and intercept course?"

"At our present course and speed, Sierra, Charlie fourteen is going to cross our path in 29 minutes."

"Bridge, aye."

The Navigator, Lieutenant Henderson, looked at where the *USS Grand Junction* was and noted that where the ship would intercept the freighter put the ship in a narrow channel between several islands. The channel didn't give the ships enough room to maneuver around if something happened. Lieutenant Henderson decided to kindly remind the captain that the pirates often struck in such narrow water channels. She picked up the phone and called the bridge.

"Navigation, bridge," said Lieutenant Henderson.

"Bridge, aye."

"Captain, recommend strongly against a boarding in that area we are heading into."

"Why?"

"Narrow channel between those islands up ahead leaves us with almost no maneuverability room. If we or that ship were attacked in that narrow channel, we could not fire back before the pirates disappeared, sir."

"Concern noted, navigator. Prepare a boarding party any way, XO."

"Yes, sir."

The freighter was boarded and nothing was found. The *USS Grand Junction* went on her way once again. As the third night was falling, the Libyan cargo carrier was moving closer to the United States. Now five days into her journey, the captain of the ship called the missile crew personnel into his cabin. The captain closed and locked the door behind them and opened up his safe. Once the captain had removed the safe's contents, he closed the safe back up again. The captain handed the missile crew personnel each a three ring binder. He further instructed them that the programming of the missiles to the FM radio stations along the east and gulf coasts of the United States was to begin tonight. The men all left the captain's cabin and headed for the cargo holds.

At the beginning of the 10th day at sea for the *USS Grand Junction,* everyone on the ship was starting to get discouraged with this law enforcement duty assignment. As night was falling, yet another set of yachts, cargo carriers, freighters and one fishing boat had been stopped and boarded. All were found to be operating their vessels properly and in accordance with International Maritime Law. The weapons officer was on the bridge talking to the captain, whom he had just relieved.

"Captain, we must look ridiculous out here chasing our tails around in circles like some dog. I want to blow something up," said the weapons officer, excitedly.

"I understand. Do you run drills on your people?"

"Yes, sir and we meet or beat the standard for this class of ships, sir."

"That's good to know; now I'm going to bed."

"Yes, sir."

The captain departed the bridge and the weapons officer started to drink his cup of coffee he had picked up before coming to the bridge. He thought it would be another uneventful night, but that was soon to change. The ship's massive array of military radarscopes picked up the pirates.

It was the electronic counter warfare crew who caught the blip on their equipment. The duty electronic counter warfare technician watched as the blip became three separate ones. Each blip had a different frequency emanating from it. The frequencies were of such output that civilian communications and radars would be effectively jammed. After a few more minutes of this, the computer, which had started to track all these blips, had narrowed the blips down to a 20 nautical mile area. There was a freighter in the zone. The duty electronic counter warfare technician surmised that this freighter was going to be their target of opportunity. Electronic counter warfare was part of the operations department and was often referred to as ECW. The operator picked up the phone and called combat.

"ECW, Combat," said the technician.

"Combat, aye," replied the duty operations officer.

"Respectfully request that you notify the bridge to set communications level delta."

"Combat, aye. Combat, Bridge."

"Bridge, aye," responded the weapons officer, who was serving as the Officer of the Deck.

"ECW just informed me to set communications level delta."

"Very well. Boatswain's Mate of the Watch, notify all departments to set communications level delta now."

"Aye, sir."

Within minutes, the *USS Grand Junction* was silent as a tomb. With no incoming transmissions with the exception of flash message traffic and only passive outgoing transmissions, the ship was like a hole on the water. The weapons officer had the messenger of the watch wake up the captain and the executive officer. Once the weapons officer had been properly relieved by the captain, he poked his head into the ECW room.

He saw three technicians using various triangulation methods to find out whom the three blips were paralleling. The three blips were paralleling the freighter. Finally the patience paid off, the ECW crew identified the blips as fast attack boats. Picking up the phone, the senior ECW technician called combat for a positive identification with passive radar.

"ECW, Combat," said the ECW technician.

"Combat, aye."

"Request positive target identification. My computer says the three blips at bearing 275 are fast attack boats."

"One moment."

There was a long pause before the combat people called back. The captain and executive officer were staring out across the starlit surface of the ocean. They were both waiting nervously since the weapons officer's debrief had included the setting of communications level delta. Again, patience paid off.

"Combat, ECW."

"ECW, aye."

"Target identification confirmed by passive radar analysis. Combat, bridge."

The captain was instantly awakened by the sound. He picked up the phone receiver from above his chair on the bridge and spoke into it.

"Bridge, aye."

"Target identification has been confirmed by passive radar analysis of the other ships' electronic transmissions. Three fast attack boats of unknown configuration and origin are closing in fast on surface contact Sierra, Charlie nineteen. These gunboats are using jamming devices, sir."

"Bridge, aye. Navigator."

"Yes, sir?"

"Plot me a parallel speed course. I want to surprise those ships."

"Yes, sir. One moment."

A few minutes went by while the navigator and the duty quartermaster went over their charts. As the pirates closed in on their next victim, the *USS Grand Junction* was closing in on them for the kill. The captain coolly drew his plans for the attack.

"Navigator, bridge."

"Bridge, aye."

"Recommend new course 280, speed flank. We should overtake their position in 22 minutes and if we maintain communications level delta, they won't hear us coming."

"Bridge, aye. Lee helm, set speed to flank."

"Lee helm, aye. Setting speed to flank."

"Helmsman, come to new course 280, right rudder twenty degrees."

"Helmsman, aye. Steer new course 280, right rudder at twenty degrees."

"Executive officer, sound battle stations."

"Aye, sir. Boatswain's Mate of the Watch, sound battle stations," said the executive officer.

"Aye, sir. General Quarters, general quarters, all hands man your battle stations. This is not a drill!"

The ship came to life. As weapons systems became active, the combat center fully activated the AEGIS IV series combat computer system. Once the AEGIS system was fully functional and fed all the current data, it started issuing its recommendations to the various departments.

The computer recommended lighting up the area with a star shell, as they were called, from the forward gun turret. It further recommended high explosive and high fragmentary rounds. As the ship closed in on the pirates, they were too busy looting the poor defenseless freighter. They never noticed the *USS Grand Junction* closing in for the kill. The captain sat back, with his battle helmet on and was calling the radio room when combat told him they were close to the pirate ships.

"Combat, bridge."

"Bridge, aye."

"Captain, we are within 5 nautical miles, sir."

"Bridge, aye. Lee helm, reduce speed to 5 knots."

"Lee helm, aye. Reducing speed to 5 knots."

The ship slowed down hardly leaving any disturbance on the ocean's surface. The captain changed his selector switch back to the radio room.

"Bridge, radio," said the captain.

"Radio, aye."

"Establish Bridge-to-Bridge communications with the pirate ships in one minute."

"Aye, sir."

The captain switched the selector switch to gun plot.

"Bridge, gun plot."

"Gun plot, aye. Weapons officer speaking."

"In two minutes, illuminate the area with a star shell. Do not target the civilian freighter. Target only the pirate vessels, until further notice, warning yellow, weapons tight."

"Aye, sir."

The captain switched back to radio.

"Bridge, radio."

"Radio, aye. You're on, sir."

"Thank you. Attention to hostile vessels bearing 279. This is the commanding officer of the warship 144, surrender and prepare to be boarded. Acknowledge this transmission in accordance with International Law."

"Screw you, sir of the warship 144. You won't fire on us," said a voice in response.

"Very well, then I will explain it in terms you understand."

The captain cut off communications and turned the switch back to gun plot.

"Bridge, gun plot."

"Gun plot, aye."

"Weapons officer, I want you to fire a shot across the bow of the two leading pirate ships after you have fired your star shell. I want you to make it close to the lead ship."

"How close do you want it?" snickered the weapons officer.

"15 to 20 meters should be sufficient."

"Yes, sir."

The *USS Grand Junction* opened up with her forward gun turret. A star shell exited the middle barrel and lit up the ocean around the ship very brightly. The next two shots from the forward turret landed the high explosive rounds 20 meters off the bows of the two forward most pirate ships.

The water boiled around the pirate ships and they took off firing as they sped off into the night. Panic and desperation set in on the pirate ships. As they made their stand against the U.S. Navy warship, they started firing small mortar rounds and chain guns in the general direction of the *USS Grand Junction.* They were trying to flee from the massive warship.

One of the pirate ships dropped a surprise into the water in its wake. The pirate ship had dropped an old Mark-45 torpedo in the water. As the *USS Grand Junction* continued in pursuit, the sonar crew picked up the torpedo. They quickly identified it as an old style Mark-45. Picking up the phone that was next to the sonar equipment, the sonar technician calmly called the bridge.

"Sonar, bridge," said the sonar crewman.

"Bridge, aye."

"Torpedo in the water, bearing 274!"

"Bridge, aye. Counter measures and evasive maneuvers."

"Aye, sir," replied the weapons officer as he pushed a button from his fire control center. The ship dropped several Mark-189 noisemakers into the water to deceive the torpedo. As this was happening, the captain turned the ship to starboard.

"Helmsman, hard to starboard!" said the captain.

"Helmsman, aye. Hard to starboard."

The warship's bow swung around to the starboard side. The torpedo missed the ship by several meters. As the warship continued its pursuit, the crew of the civilian freighter was being treated to a wonderful spectacle. The warship's turrets would open fire and illuminate the ship briefly. The freighter crew knew that this would be a sight to never be forgotten.

By now the pirates were running wildly about, running low on ammunition and fuel. One of the pirate ships turned the wrong direction and the 8-inch, high explosive round, hit the bridge. The ship was totally destroyed, sinking immediately.

"Combat, bridge."

"Bridge, aye."

"One pirate ship confirmed sunk. The ship apparently turned directly into the trajectory path of the second gun turret's salvo. That pirate ship's bearing was 299."

"Bridge, aye. Captain, we inadvertently sunk the pirate ship bearing 299. Combat reports that the pirate ship inadvertently turned directly into the path of the oncoming salvo from gun turret number two."

"Thank you, XO. Continue firing and pursuit," responded the captain.

"Aye, sir."

The pirate ships, now only numbering two, looked at their empty magazines and their nearly empty fuel tanks. With no more ammunition and no more torpedoes, the first mate of the pirate ship *Kidd* looked at the captain. The look of fear was showing heavily in his eyes.

"Captain, if that warship hits us with their artillery shells, they will destroy us just like they did *Charlie Company*."

"I think you're right. Stop all engines and signal our surrender. I believe we might fare better in the criminal justice system than with the warship."

"Aye, sir."

The first mate shut down the engines and signaled to the other boat to come alongside and tie up. The captain of the other pirate boat agreed that surrendering to the warship was, under the present circumstances, the better part of valor. As the boats came to a stop, the first mate fired a white flare into the air and then called the warship on Bridge-to-Bridge transmission.

"To the warship 144, this is the first mate of the pirate ship *Kidd;* we surrender," he said solemnly.

"Radio, bridge," said the radioman on duty.

"Bridge, aye."

"The first mate of the pirate ship *Kidd* is signaling their surrender. Their current position is bearing 296."

"Bridge, aye. Put me through to him."

"Aye, sir. You're on."

"Surrender is hereby acknowledged by the commanding officer of the warship 144. In accordance with the United Nations Sea Charter of 1949 as amended, prepare to be boarded and taken into custody by the authority granted to me in paragraph 175," said the captain of the *USS Grand Junction.*

"We concur."

"XO, cease fire! Boatswain's Mate of the Watch, have the ship's Master-at-Arms prepare the brig for detainees and muster an armed boarding security detail."

"Aye, sir."

The ship stopped firing her 8-inch guns. Searchlights were used to light up the area now. In all, fourteen pirates were taken into custody. The weapons, equipment and boats were all seized in accordance with International Law. The captain of the *USS Grand Junction* had his deck crews secure the pirate boats with two ropes. The captains of both pirate ships were being held in separate cells for security reasons. The crews were being held in separate cells as well.

The ship secured from general quarters and four hours later they were anchored off the coast of a small Caribbean island. The local law enforcement authorities ran boats out to get the pirates. While they waited for further orders, the ship remained anchored in the bay area, taking on some provisions.

The captain of the ship spent the rest of the morning writing up his report and preparing it for transmission. When the report was finished, he sent the report off in message format to the Commander-in-Chief of Atlantic Fleet Forces. On the message, the captain made sure that the admiral was made aware that in accordance with his explicit orders, law enforcement duties were being terminated at this time. The message also clearly stated that the ship had not sustained any serious damage except from some mortar and small arms fire on the starboard side hull. That damage was nothing more than cosmetic with the deck crew quickly repainting the ship. He further requested for a few days down time for maintenance and evaluation of the weapons systems.

# Chapter 10

The message from the *USS Grand Junction* was received a little after 0900 hours Eastern Standard Time. The radio room decoded the priority message and turned it over to Admiral Jamison. Admiral Jamison read the nine-page message and smiled. No serious damage to the ship, only a minor paint job. Putting the message down on his desktop, he picked up the phone to call Admiral Nagomu. Admiral Nagomu's secretary answered the phone.

"Yes, YN2 Brown this is Admiral Jamison. I need to speak with Admiral Nagomu."

"One moment, sir."

Admiral Jamison was put on hold for a short period of time while YN2 Brown tracked down Admiral Nagomu. Admiral Nagomu had told YN2 Brown that if any important calls came in for him, that Admiral Nagomu would be inside the Pentagon building or at the White House. YN2 Brown located Admiral Nagomu at the White House.

The White House switchboard operator told YN2 Brown that the admiral was in a meeting with the Secretary of Homeland Security and the Secretary of Transportation. Also present at this meeting was the Director of the CIA. A page came into the meeting and whispered into Admiral Nagomu's left ear. Admiral Nagomu politely excused himself from the meeting to take the call.

"Yes, YN2 Brown, what can I do for you?" asked Admiral Nagomu.

"I have Admiral Jamison on the line for you, sir."

"Excellent, put him through."

"Yes, sir. I am transferring the call right now."

During the transfer of the call, Admiral Nagomu grabbed a pen and a pad of paper to write down anything of interest from Admiral Jamison.

"Admiral Nagomu, I received a priority message about 15 minutes ago from the commanding officer of the *USS Grand Junction.* He states in his message that he has impounded two fast attack gunboats and arrested fourteen pirates."

"That's very good news, Admiral Jamison. Was there any reported damage to the ship?"

"Only minor cosmetic damage to the starboard side. The captain reports that the deck crews are repainting the starboard side right now. He is asking for some down time for an evaluation of this evolution. As far as the pirates are concerned, they are in the custody of that island government."

"Downtime granted of 72 hours. How many rounds were fired?"

"32 rounds were fired and the captain reported that three countermeasures were used to deceive a torpedo that was fired at them."

"That torpedo didn't hit the ship, did it?"

"No, sir and even if it did, that nine inches of solid armor plate could take it quite well. The captain reported to me that the sonar crew detected and classified the torpedo before it could even threaten the ship in any manner. The torpedo was left over from Vietnam I believe. It was an old Mark-45 C series."

"Any casualties?"

"One. Apparently one of the pirate boats went to evade a shot that had been fired from the ship. The captain reports that the pirate boat turned directly into the oncoming shot and was sunk; no survivors."

"Excellent. Thank you for your report and see to it that the ship gets some sort of commendation citation or a meritorious unit citation medal."

"I will, sir."

"Where is the ship now?"

"Anchored off the coast of some small island down there. Apparently the island's piers cannot handle something that big. The ship is currently taking on provisions."

"Okay, at least I know where the ship is. Admiral Jamison, see to it that, at the earliest possible time, the ship gets rearmed; good-bye."

"Yes Admiral Nagomu, I will see to it that the ship gets rearmed and have a nice day," said Admiral Jamison, hanging up the phone.

Admiral Nagomu returned to the meeting. He passed along the information to the President. The President gave the okay to the Secretary of Homeland Security to lower the threat level from Orange to Yellow. When the meeting broke up, everyone thought that any danger to the United States was over. They were unaware of the important message that was yet to be received from Michael Pigeon.

Meanwhile, the cargo carrier, maintaining a steady course and speed, inched closer to the east coast of the United States. As night was falling on the cargo carrier, the captain asked for a briefing in his stateroom. He instructed the missile crew personnel to double-check the missile's fuel supplies. He wanted to make sure that the missiles were going to make it to their targets. They all celebrated the fact that they were going to "kill as many of the infidels" as they could in one attack. This attack, if successful, would be much bigger than September 11, 2001 in New York City, Washington D.C. and Pennsylvania.

The message that Michael had written before he died was collecting dust on the tabletop in the chart room of the billionaire's yacht. When the billionaire was pier side in Brest, France for fuel and provisions, he went looking for a fax machine. With message in hand, he located a fax machine within a few kilometers of where his yacht was docked. Stepping inside the small store, he approached the customer service counter with the eight-page message. A young man stood up from behind the counter and greeted the billionaire.

"Good day, sir. Can I help you with anything?" he asked in English, with a heavy French accent.

"How much to send a fax?" he asked.

"Where to, sir?"

"The United States of America."

"Thirty U.S. dollars for the first page and twenty-five U.S. dollars for every page thereafter."

"Please fax this to area code 303-696-2773," he said, handing the man the eight-page message.

"Yes, sir."

When the fax was completed and paid for, the pages started to print out on Bill's desk. Bill wasn't available to take the fax because he was in a meeting in Washington D.C. He was getting out of the meeting and stepping on board the State Department jet as the sun was setting. He arrived late back to Denver, Colorado. His heart was heavy with the reported death of SPOT agent Michael Pigeon. This death report was fresh on the minds of all the SPOT support personnel worldwide when the Secretary of State decided to add salt to a still open wound.

During the meeting, the Secretary of State had decided to disband the SPOT personnel. By the beginning of October, all State Department SPOT units and their associated personnel were to be reassigned, retired or released. Bill fought to keep the SPOT unit for Denver, Colorado; in the end, the Secretary of State decided that for budget reasons, it would be better to eliminate the SPOT program. Bill left the meeting and came back to Denver, Colorado. He opened up his office door and entered into his office. He turned on the desk lamp and sat down at his desk. As he rubbed his tired, bloodshot eyes, he caught sight of the green flashing light on the fax machine.

Bill stood up and walked over to the fax machine. The green blinking light told Bill that the fax machine was out of paper. The fax machine went on to state that it had more faxes in its memory to print. Bill opened the paper tray door and loaded two full reams of paper into the fax machine. When he shut the paper tray door, the fax machine said "Thank you."

The fax machine then started to print up the remaining pages that were stored in its memory. When the fax machine went back to being quiet, Bill decided to read the fax that had just arrived. Bill grabbed the eight-page fax and sat down at his desk, pouring himself a drink in the process.

Bill read the fax with great concern and then set it down on the desktop. He quickly picked up the phone. He looked through his phone listing for the private home phone number for the Secretary of Homeland Security. Bill dialed the number and the phone rang several times before the Secretary of Homeland Security, half awake, answered the phone. It was Saturday morning for the Secretary.

"Secretary of Homeland Security," he said yawning.

"Yes, sir. This is Bill Yancy and I just received a fax on my desk sent from Brest, France earlier this morning. It's from Michael Pigeon and he discovered something before his death."

"What did he discover, Bill?"

"The Libyans put to sea a cargo carrier, which I have all the data on, with several hundred Al-Fatah II series missiles. The rest of the information I cannot tell you unless we are on a secure line."

"Jesus Christ, Bill. If the information is that important that you saw fit to wake me up at 0430 hours on a Saturday morning, then give me the damned information."

"I'm sorry, sir. Regulations are specific; sensitive information cannot be released through unsecured transmitting devices. This includes the telephone that we are talking on right now."

"Very well, can you at least give me some basic idea of this information?" he asked.

"Basically, the information spells out that the Libyans are planning an attack on the United States as retribution, sir."

"I'll call the President. Fax all the information you have to area code 202-456-9494. I'll meet with the President at the White House; Bill, keep this quiet."

"Yes, sir. Sorry to have woken you up."

Bill hung up the phone and faxed the eight-page fax to the number that he was given. The fax printed out and was waiting on the Secretary of Homeland Security when he arrived at the White House. The President was still getting dressed and trying to wake up. The Director of the CIA was arriving and was still trying to wake up. The Secretary of Homeland Security put on his reading glasses, which he had put into his left shirt pocket before leaving his house and read the fax. He handed the fax over to the Director of the CIA and then the fax was handed to the President.

"Holy dog crap, is this fax real or a hoax?" asked the Director of the CIA.

"That printing looks real and I believe, after having seen Michael Pigeon's handwriting enough times, that the information is from his own hand. Michael must have stumbled onto this project of the Libyans just before he died," replied the Secretary of Homeland Security.

The President read the fax and set it down on the tabletop. He took in a deep breath and let it out slowly. His eyes were closed as he massaged the temples of his head. He opened his eyes and spoke slowly.

"Just how many people know about this fax?" asked the President.

"Just us in this room and Mr. Yancy," replied the Secretary of Homeland Security.

"Good. If this information is real, then we have only a few more hours to intercept this cargo carrier. You all realize that we are looking at threat level Red if this planned attack becomes a reality," said the President.

"Yes, sir, I realize that is a possibility. Unfortunately, this information came from a corpse, so we cannot ascertain if it is accurate," said the Director of the CIA.

"You don't think the information is accurate, Mr. Director?" asked the President.

"No, I don't think the information is accurate. The information came from someone who was dying. There is a chance that maybe he hallucinated all this and wrote it down believing it to be real."

"Okay. What is your opinion on the validity of the information, Mr. Secretary of Homeland Security?" asked the President directly to him.

"Let's consider four key points of information in this message. One, we know that in the past, Libya has been responsible, at least indirectly, for terrorist attacks on all nations; Pan-Am Flight 103. This fax clearly states the Libyans intent to attack the United States, specifically the east and gulf coasts. This attack is being carried out by them as a jihad against the infidels as they refer to us."

"Okay, so far. What other points do you claim to make this information credible and real?" asked the Director of the CIA.

"Second, Michael gives us a complete list of what is in the cargo carrier's cargo holds. Including the blast deflector plating and other items that he found. He could not have possibly known this information without having been aboard that ship," replied the Secretary of Homeland Security.

"That's true and valid," commented the President.

"Third, Michael gives us a complete description of the cargo carrier. Answer this question, Mr. Director of the CIA, how come this cargo carrier needed to be armor plated?" asked the Secretary of Homeland Security.

"Good point. Maybe the armor plating was going to allow the ship to survive a heavy attack by our navy," replied the Director of the CIA, with all sorts of alarm bells going off in his mind.

"Fourth, Michael is able to estimate the ship's speed and course. Plus he provides us with at least a partial list of intended targets. Without being on the cargo carrier and being underway with it, he would not have been able to provide us with this type of detailed information."

"In other words, we have three options, none of which I like. Option one, this message is a fake coming from a man suffering from the effects of radiation poisoning and is probably a happy hallucination. Option two, we go to full military alert status and put the country at threat level Red over an event that may or may not happen. Option three, we wait to be attacked with our defenses down and then shoot back at, hopefully, the right target," said the President.

"Yes, sir, that is the basics of the issues. However, I am about to share with you, Mr. President, some intelligence information that was sent to us by Michael Pigeon before he died. This information is, of course, classified as Sensitive," said the Director of the CIA.

"What Sensitive intelligence information are you referring to?" asked the President, rather surprised.

"We have pictures that show some equipment in a room that was used to make nuclear warheads. The equipment in the pictures is very outdated and is no longer used and has been declassified for full public release. The equipment was used to make the first atomic bombs that we used in World War II. Over time, the equipment was found to be less than safe. Soon, much better equipment was built to make nuclear warheads safer and more efficient,"

"I thought the Libyans denounced their nuclear program in 2003," said the President.

"Yes, they did, sir. However, they may have nuclear weapons in the form of the Al-Fatah II series missiles," replied the Director of the CIA.

"Could somebody tell me what this missile is capable of?" asked the President.

"The Al-Fatah II series missile is 40 percent larger than its predecessor, the Al-Fatah I series missile. Both missiles are classified as Intermediate Range Ballistic Missiles. The Al-Fatah I series missile can only carry a 500 kilogram payload between 950 to 1,100 nautical miles," said the Secretary of Homeland Security.

"So, this upgraded missile could be worse?" asked the President.

"Yes, sir. The Al-Fatah II series missile normally carries a 2,000-kilogram payload between 1,100 to an estimated 1,300 nautical miles. However, there is the distinct probability that this newer missile could carry up to a 500 kiloton tactical nuclear warhead," said the Director of the CIA.

"Oh my God, do we have anything that big in our arsenal?" asked the President.

"No, sir. I believe our arsenal only has a 250-kiloton tactical nuclear warhead on a cruise missile. I believe that we use this tactical nuclear warhead as some sort of bunker buster," replied the Director of the CIA.

"However, sir, your predecessor gave the orders to develop larger tactical nuclear warheads for destroying deep underground bunkers," said the Secretary of Homeland Security.

"A 500 kiloton tactical nuclear warhead could do some serious damage to a major city. The Libyans supposedly have these missiles and they are possibly nuclear armed?" asked the President for clarification purposes.

"Yes, sir," said the Director of the CIA.

"So, this threat may be all the more real, sir. Unlike my colleague across the table, I think this information is very credible and needs to be treated as such. Mr. President, I respectfully request that as of 1200 hours today, you need to put the country at threat level Red," said the Secretary of Homeland Security.

"Why wait until then?" asked the President.

"Two reasons, sir. One, there is no reason to start a panic over something that may be false. This leeway time gives me a chance to bring my department to maximum alert status. Second, it gives the flexibility of still being able to destroy this cargo carrier before the ship can strike us," said the Secretary of Homeland Security.

"Alright, I'll call Admiral Young and get something going. Mr. Director of the CIA, you have until 1130 hours to determine if this fax is a fake or a hoax before I call a press conference."

"Understood, sir. I'll get started on it right away."

The Director of the CIA got onto the phone right away, notifying his various department heads of the situation and instructing them as to exactly what needed to be done. He told them when the last possible minute would be and they agreed to have an answer by then. The Director of the CIA then stood up and excused himself. Now it was only the President and Secretary of Homeland Security in the room.

"Mr. Secretary, mobilize your forces. Tell them it is a drill until further notice," said the President.

"Yes, sir I will start the preparations."

"Good. I'll call Admiral Young of my Joint Chiefs of Staff and pass along this information. This was a very clever plan. The Libyans knew it would be tough on me to issue the orders to sink civilian shipping. Very clever, indeed. Dismissed," said the President.

Meanwhile, having completed taking on provisions and having completed the gunfire exercise evaluation, the *USS Grand Junction* set the sea and anchor detail at 0430 hours Eastern Standard Time. At 0445 hours, Eastern Standard Time, the ship was underway. The course that had been plotted was taking the ship back home to the Norfolk Naval Base. As the sun rose higher into the sky, the ship cruised at 14 knots in the Cobalt blue waters of the Caribbean, headed into the Atlantic. The sea was relatively calm and the ship rocked back and forth gently in the two to three foot swells.

Meanwhile, back in Washington D.C., Admiral Young of the Joint Chiefs of Staff had received his briefing and orders from the President. He shook hands with the President and left the White House. He was headed immediately to the Pentagon building to make some phone calls.

When he arrived at the Chief of Naval Operations office, he found out that Admiral Nagomu was not there. His secretary, YN2 Brown, said that Admiral Nagomu was in Norfolk, Virginia. Admiral Nagomu was supposedly at the office of the Commander-in-chief of Atlantic Fleet Forces Admiral Jamison Commanding. Admiral Young continued down to his office and used his secure phone to call Admiral Jamison on the admiral's secure phone line.

The red phone started ringing on Admiral Jamison's desktop. Admiral Nagomu looked at Admiral Jamison and raised his eyebrows up a little. Admiral Atwell looked curiously at Admiral Jamison to see if Admiral Jamison would answer the phone or not. Nervously, Admiral Jamison picked up the receiver. Putting the receiver up to his ear, he spoke slowly and clearly.

"Commander-in-chief Atlantic Fleet Forces, Admiral Jamison speaking," he said.

"Yes, Admiral Jamison. This is Admiral Young of the Joint Chiefs of Staff calling. I understand that Admiral Nagomu and possibly Admiral Atwell are present with you," said Admiral Young.

"Yes, sir, that is correct," said Admiral Jamison, looking across the desktop at Admirals Nagomu and Atwell.

"Good, that will save time. Put me on the speaker phone."

"Yes, sir."

Admiral Jamison pushed the button in on the speakerphone as he placed the receiver back into its cradle.

"Go ahead, Admiral Young," said Admiral Jamison.

"Thank you and you all might want to take some notes. I have received a threat briefing from the President. It appears that the Libyans have outfitted a civilian cargo carrier to be a floating missile launcher. I have the specifics for you and the other admirals to pass along to the various ship commanders."

As Admiral Young went to speak, Admiral Jamison handed several pens and some notepads across his desktop to the other admirals. Everyone started taking notes. Admiral Young paused until he heard no more writing on the notepads.

"The President, at 1200 hours today, is going to put the entire country at threat level Red due to this threat. The Libyans apparently manufactured several hundred 500-kiloton tactical nuclear warheads. These nuclear warheads are attached to Al-Fatah II series missiles. The President wants the following action from the navy."

He paused again until he heard the sound of pen to paper stop.

"One, no civilian shipping is to be within 1,300 nautical miles of the east coast of the United States without having first been checked and cleared. Two, any ship that is not compliant with directive one shall be challenged and interrogated thoroughly. Three, any civilian shipping that launches missiles shall be sunk immediately. Four, the U.S. Coast Guard will help out as best they can by providing radar coverage and other services."

He could hear a lot of writing; again, he waited until it stopped before continuing.

"Here are the hostile ship specifics. The ship is heavily armor plated with at least six inches of armor plate. The information that was given to me states that at least the hull has six inches of armor plating. The information does not say anything about the superstructure; assume it is also that thickly armor plated."

The admiral waited until the writing had stopped again.

"The ship's last known course was estimated at 273. The ship had an estimated speed of 18 knots with six days travel time. She will be within earliest launch range of those missiles at 1245 hours Eastern Standard Time. We have calculated that the latest possible launch time would be 1330 hours Eastern Standard Time."

He waited again until all the pens had stopped writing.

"That puts the ship within 315 nautical miles of the U.S. east coast. The U.S. must be protected at all costs. You have your orders, get these orders out on flash message traffic."

"Yes, sir," replied Admiral Jamison.

Admiral Young hung up the phone. Admiral Nagomu looked at Admiral Jamison. Admiral Jamison looked at Admiral Atwell. Admiral Jamison finally broke the silence in the room by standing up and looking over his ship's status board.

He then looked at the map of the east coast of the United States that he had hanging up on his wall in his office. The area to be covered was enormous, even with the help of the Coast Guard. Admiral Jamison knew that it would be almost impossible to carry out such a task. The ship's status board showed one battle group ready for deployment, one destroyer and one cruiser squadron each ready; only 30 ships capable of anti-ship duty.

Admiral Jamison figured it would be well past 1800 hours before any of those ships could be within striking distance with their cruise missiles. Admiral Jamison even knew that with boosters on those missiles it would be, at the earliest, 1700 hours Eastern Standard Time before he had anything ready. As he looked at Admiral Atwell, Admiral Jamison started to smile.

"Admiral Nagomu, tell Admiral Young that I will deploy all of my available ships that are anti-ship capable. I will also try and get in touch with my submarines in the designated area as well," said Admiral Jamison.

"Okay, I will let him know," replied Admiral Nagomu.

As Admiral Jamison looked at the ship's status board once more, he saw a flag down in the Caribbean. Looking at the area to protect once again, he saw that there was one ship that was anti-ship capable and within striking distance. He turned to Admiral Atwell.

"Admiral Atwell, what is the current status and weapons inventory of CA-144?" asked Admiral Jamison.

"CA-144, at last report, was underway this morning at 0445 Eastern Standard Time. The ship has been cruising at 14 knots on a course of 020 for the last five hours. She is fully armed minus her main armament and some countermeasures," replied Admiral Atwell.

"Isn't that ship equipped with the new upgraded TOMA-HAWK's?"

"Yes, sir. Those TOMAHAWK cruise missiles are now equipped with an experimental 2,000 kilogram payload."

"Admiral Atwell, you are a very clever man. The *USS Grand Junction* could be within striking distance by 1145 hours Eastern Standard Time at flank speed. The ship's crew could start outfitting the Tomahawk's with boosters to extend their range. Is there any way to contact the commanding officer directly?" asked Admiral Jamison.

"Yes, sir, Admiral Jamison. We can go to the radio room and I will get the radio operators to establish a direct link to the ship via INMARSAT," replied Admiral Atwell.

"Okay, let's do it. Sorry, Admiral Nagomu, that our golf game was cancelled," said Admiral Jamison.

"That's okay, I will be returning to Washington, D.C. now," said Admiral Nagomu as he left the office.

Admiral Nagomu quickly left the building, heading for the Norfolk Naval Air Station where his plane was located. Admiral Jamison walked with Admiral Atwell to the base radio communications center. Admiral Atwell had the duty radio center operator establish communications with the commanding officer of the *USS Grand Junction*. Once the particulars were handled, the crew of the ship prepared for a very important mission to protect the home front. After having completed the INMARSAT phone conversation, the captain stepped out onto the bridge and issued orders.

"Lee helm, set your speed to flank," said the captain.

"Aye, sir, flank speed," said the seaman apprentice at the lee helm station.

"Helmsman, come to new course 045,"

"Aye, sir. Coming to new course 045," replied the helmsman.

"Boatswain's Mate of the Watch, pass the word for an all officers meeting in the wardroom in five minutes."

"Aye, sir."

The captain left the bridge. In charge of the bridge now was the Supply Officer. He looked at all the digital readouts to confirm their new course and speed. The captain gave the briefing to the officers. The missile crews started equipping at least three of their cruise missiles with boosters. This gave the cruise missile a range of up to 650 nautical miles. This evolution would take several hours.

The captain passed along the information about the enemy ship to the navigator. After the meeting was over, the navigator set out to calculate where the cargo carrier might be. The calculations narrowed the search area to a 500 nautical mile area. As the navigator tried his best to narrow the search area further, the captain of the cargo carrier was opening the cargo hatches.

The captain of the cargo carrier reviewed the ship's navigational lines once again. At 1050 hours, Eastern Standard Time, the ship was to turn to course 184. The ship was to stay on this course for one hour. At 1150 hours, the ship was to turn to a more northwest course of 348. This would allow the ship to parallel the Florida coast pretty close to shore. He knew that at 1215 hours, the ship could start launching the missiles and even if the U.S. Navy sunk them, their missiles, on self-guidance to the FM radio stations, would make it to their targets.

Meanwhile, aboard the *USS Grand Junction* the captain and the Fire Control Officer, Ensign Delmonte, agreed that if the cargo carrier were armor plated, with six inches of it, and not knowing if the superstructure was so outfitted, that it might survive one missile hit. They planned to fire a second cruise missile 20 seconds after the first one.

This cruise missile would have a loiter path of 45 seconds before hitting the cargo carrier again. The Fire Control Officer informed the captain that he could have the second cruise missile strike the ship at any time before the end of the loiter time. The captain would keep closing the distance to the cargo carrier and strike the cargo carrier again if needed. The Fire Control Officer decided to try and equip three TOMAHAWK cruise missiles with boosters, but the captain said that there wasn't enough time for that. The captain did agree that a third TOMAHAWK could be fired 45 minutes after the other two.

The navigator was becoming very frustrated with trying to narrow down the search area and was ready to give it up, when the newest Quartermaster, QM3 Quincy, set his charts and notebook down on the chart table. The navigator looked up at him strangely.

"Sir, I think I can narrow down the search area to maybe as little as 50 nautical miles," said QM3 Quincy.

"How's that, QM3 Quincy?" asked the navigator.

"We know that the enemy ship has been on an estimated course of 273, with an estimated speed of 18 knots for at least six days travel time," he said, using a black grease marking pencil to show the navigator what he was talking about on the charts he had set down earlier.

"Okay, go ahead."

"That means the enemy ship could, at any one of three points of time, take any one of three different courses to attack the U.S.," he said, pointing at the shipping lane tracks on the charts.

"I'm with you so far," said the navigator.

At this time, QM3 Quincy pulled out his notebook, which contained all of his calculations.

"If I were the skipper of that ship and I wanted to draw as little attention to myself as possible, but I wanted to maximize my missile's flight distance, I would choose the southern route on a course of 348."

"Why?"

"The southern route would be least traveled and it would bring my ship to within 315 nautical miles of the eastern coast of Florida. Once I launch my missiles, by the time they are picked up on radar, my ship won't be anywhere near the estimated trajectory path launch area."

"Okay, how would I intercept this ship?"

"According to my calculations, we would have to change course to 005 at 1015 hours. At 1045 hours, we would have to change course to 358. At 1130 hours, we would have to change course to 340. If the other ship turns into this southern route, like I project the ship will, then we should have no problem singling out the ship up on our radar at or about 1145 hours. I estimate that the cruise missiles should reach their target by 1159 hours."

The navigator looked up at the ship's clock and back down at the chart table. He picked up the phone and called the bridge.

"Navigation, Bridge," said the navigator.

"Bridge, aye," responded the captain.

"Recommend coming to new course 005 at 1015 hours. Please see me in the chart room."

"Bridge, aye," replied the captain, putting the phone back up.

"Helmsman, come to new course 005."

"Aye, sir, coming to new course 005."

"XO, you have the bridge. I'll be in the chart room."

"Aye, sir."

The captain left the bridge and entered the chart room.

"What do you have for me, navigator?" asked the captain.

"QM3 Quincy, here, thinks he as the answer to your question of where the enemy ship might be," said the navigator.

QM3 Quincy repeated himself to the captain. The captain asked a few more questions than what the navigator had asked, but the captain seemed pleased with the plan. The captain left the chart room and stopped by combat. The combat radar operators were having a tough time.

"How many targets on the scopes?" asked the captain.

"I have 30 total, sir," said the Operations Officer.

"Narrow it down to just cargo carriers," said the captain.

"Seven, sir."

"Well, here's some advice. Look for the cargo carrier who might turn to course 184 at or about 1050 hours. Then look for another course change to 348 thereafter."

"Yes, sir."

The captain returned to the bridge and waited. At 1045 hours, the *USS Grand Junction* made its last turn to course 340. As the ship swung its bow around to its new course, the radar operators watched as the number of ships dropped by ten. Now, only three cargo carriers were present. The Operations Officer watched as two of the cargo carriers turned to new courses 090 and 155. The third cargo carrier stayed on its original course and speed. At 1050 hours, the Operations Officer watched as the third cargo carrier started turning to a new course of 184. The Operations Officer picked up the phone and called the bridge.

"Combat, bridge," said the Operations Officer.

The captain picked up the phone.

"Bridge, aye."

"Radar indicates that contact Sierra, Sierra, Charlie Four has changed to course 184."

"Bridge, aye."

The captain switched the selector switch to fire control.

"Bridge, Fire Control."

"Fire Control, aye," responded the Fire Control Officer.

"Begin tracking and prepare the TOMAHAWK guidance systems. Your target tracker assignment is Sierra, Sierra, Charlie four."

"Fire Control, aye."

"Call me back when you have a positive target lock."

"Aye, sir."

All the captain could do now was wait.

Meanwhile, the captain of the cargo carrier increased his speed. The cargo hatches were fully open now. All the Al-Fatah II series missiles were seeing the light of day for the first time in many years. The increase in speed however was detected by combat aboard the *USS Grand Junction.*

"Combat, Bridge," said the Operations Officer.

"Bridge, aye," responded the captain.

"Contact Sierra, Sierra, Charlie four has increased speed to 21 knots."

"Bridge, aye."

"Fire Control, Bridge."

"Bridge, aye."

"I have confirmed a positive target lock on Sierra, Sierra, Charlie four."

"Bridge, aye. What is the estimated flight time of the missiles?"

"Estimated flight time is 13 minutes, 26 seconds on missile one. Missile two is set for a 20-second delayed launch and a 45 second loiter path."

"Bridge, aye. Fire Control, prepare to launch those missiles."

"Aye, sir."

The deck forward of the first gun turret was cleared of all personnel. Two hatches on the vertical launch tubes five and six were opened up. The TOMAHAWK anti-ship cruise missiles were redesigned and upgraded. Each cruise missile was carrying a 2,000-kilogram payload at a speed of two and half times the speed of sound and eagerly greeted the afternoon sun. The missiles were readied for their flight. At 1130 hours, the *USS Grand Junction* made the final turn. The other ship made its final turn as well.

"Combat, Bridge," said the Operations Officer.

"Bridge, aye," responded the captain.

"Contact Sierra, Sierra, Charlie four has changed course to 349 and has decreased speed to five knots."

"Bridge, aye. Fire Control, Bridge," said the captain.

"Fire Control, aye."

"There has been a slight change in plans. Recalculate flight time of the missiles since target has decreased speed to five knots."

"Fire Control, aye. First missile now estimated impact nine minutes after launch. I will have the other missile launch 10 seconds after the first one and loiter only 10 seconds."

"Bridge, aye. Fire when ready."

"Aye, sir."

The two TOMAHAWK anti-ship cruise missiles leaped up into the air. Once their rocket engines had ignited, they left a short trail of white smoke that floated over the ship. The cruise missiles raced towards their target. The cargo carrier was not aware of the cruise missiles and was busy preparing the launching of their missiles. As the cargo carrier cruised towards the east coast of the U.S., the first cruise missile struck the ship a devastating blow.

The first TOMAHAWK hit the cargo carrier and tore through the superstructure and downward into the open cargo holds. The ship stopped suddenly in the water and explosions were going off from both the explosive payload of the TOMAHAWK and the spilled rocket fuel from the Al-Fatah II series missiles. The cargo carrier had indeed survived the first hit. The armor plating extended into the superstructure a short distance, but the cargo carrier only received a slight reprieve.

The second TOMAHAWK hit 14 seconds later. This cruise missile entered on the port side of the ship at the waterline. The explosive payload went off punching a hole all the way through the amidships cargo hold and into the forward cargo hold all the way down to the waterline. The cargo carrier didn't last long.

As the *USS Grand Junction* arrived on scene to pick up any survivors, the cargo carrier rolled over to the port side and sunk rapidly. With no survivors to pick up, the captain of the *USS Grand Junction* notified the chain of command that the ship had been destroyed. The President was notified and was greatly relieved at not having to put the country at threat level Red.

When Bill Yancy was told about the news, he was just happy that Michael Pigeon had not died in vain. Bill was happy that Michael had died to protect and defend the homeland just as Michael had been taught when he was first hired so many years ago.